SECOND WEDNESDAY

ALSO BY J.C. VAUGHN

24 OMNIBUS
(with Mark L. Haynes & others)

ANTIQUES: THE COMIC STRIP
(with Brendon & Brian Fraim)

SHI: JU-NEN
(with Billy Tucci)

STARGATE ATLANTIS – VOLUME 1
(with Mark L. Haynes & others)

STARGATE ATLANTIS – VOLUME 2
(with Mark L. Haynes & others)

STARGATE UNIVERSE – VOLUME 1
(with Mark L. Haynes & others)

VAMPIRE, PA
(with Brendon & Brian Fraim)

ZOMBIE-PROOF
(with Vincent Spencer)

SECOND WEDNESDAY

A Donovan Bay/Michelle Benson Mystery

By J.C. Vaughn

Gemstone Publishing
Hunt Valley, Maryland

Copyright ©2021 by J.C. Vaughn
Cover art ©2021 by Joe Jusko

Cover & Book Design by Dawn Guzzo / Atomic Studios

Author photo by Rosina Ally

International Rights and other queries: K_G_Bird@outlook.com

Standard Edition ISBN 978-1-60360-273-0
Deluxe Limited Edition ISBN 978-1-60360-272-3

First printing April 2021 by Gemstone Publishing, Inc.
10150 York Road, Suite 300
Hunt Valley, MD 21030
www.gemstonepub.com

Printed in Canada

To Rosina, as always.

*With special thanks to Jason Odom,
Adam Philips, Georgi Sandgren, Debbie Shocair,
Babette Welch, and Doug Zirkle.*

SECOND WEDNESDAY

CHAPTER 1

FOURTEEN MONTHS AGO

He smirked. That was the trigger.

It was as if he couldn't imagine that any malice held against him could lead him to genuine harm. After all, it had been consensual, hadn't it?

The first strike had come as a complete surprise to him.

In an upward motion, unseen until it was too late, the blade entered the abdomen, cutting into the small intestines, the transverse colon, and the stomach. It was accompanied instantly by startling and severe pain followed almost immediately by additional sensations of discomfort.

He tried to step backward, to get away, but there would be none of that. A faltering half step, and then he collapsed.

For some reason his shock, his utter surprise that this could be happening to him, enraged his attacker and unleashed an almost unimaginable fury.

The first wound was the least ferocious of the attack. Those that followed increased in both rage and blunt force before they finally began to subside. His final raspy noises went unheard by his attacker.

Then it was over, as over as it was ever going to be.

FIVE YEARS EARLIER

"Johnny Juarez, open up! Hurst Police Department," I yelled after first banging on the door. Juarez was wanted for failing to appear in court on a burglary charge. He had no history of violent offenses, and we'd definitely seen longer rap sheets, but we had our vests on and weapons ready as a matter of policy and common sense. We got no answer, but we thought we could hear noise of some kind from inside.

I tried calling out one more time. This time there was no ambiguity about the noise. Two shots came through the door, one in the middle, one higher, both of them missing us. Michael Solof and I flattened ourselves on either side of the door.

"Officers request assistance. Shots fired. Cinnamon Ridge Apartments off of Bedford Road, unit 16," Mike called it in. The reply came quickly. Hurst was not much in the way of this kind of excitement, and it was a good bet that half the force would be here in less than two minutes.

"Cover the back. It's no easy exit, but we'll just keep him here and wait for back-up," I said and motioned for Mike to turn to his left and follow the short path around the building. He nodded, but as he took his first step we heard a scream from inside.

It was a child's cry for help.

Mike cursed, froze in place, then turned around.

"I think we gotta go in, Donovan," he said.

"The door frame's ratty. It's going to give right away," I said. "You go high; I'll go low." He nodded.

I hit the door with my full force and the door frame splintered immediately. I just followed gravity to the floor.

Right inside the apartment there was a hallway that led away from the door I'd just come through. It ran back toward the main living area. About eight feet down the hall there was a closed door on the left and another about four feet after that. I could hear a television coming from what I supposed was the living room.

Three shots in quick succession came our way, one hitting the door as it swung, one embedding in the wall by the door, and the other striking Mike in the left shoulder, spinning him backward and sending him down to the concrete sidewalk.

I kept my weapon and my gaze aimed forward, but yelled to him.

"Mike?"

"Crap, that hurt," he said quietly "I'm hit, but I think the vest took most of it." Then his voice went louder as he called the update in over the radio.

"Johnny, you've still got a chance to give yourself up," I yelled down the hall.

Two more shots, both hitting the wall. Based on where they made their impact, I didn't think Juarez could see where I was on the floor.

I crawled forward to where I was beside the first door on the left. I pressed my ear to it and didn't hear anything but my own heart beating. I realized that my adrenaline was in high gear, which seemed entirely reasonable since Johnny Juarez was trying to kill me.

I backed up just a bit to use the wall as protection, then as quietly as I could I reached up, turned the doorknob, and then pushed the door open. The first thing I saw was that there were toys on the floor. A kid's bedroom. No, two kids' bedroom. Twin beds. No motion from inside. Weapon ready, I rolled in and came up standing, and saw them. One on each bed, two boys, one maybe six and the other maybe a few years older, a single gunshot wound on each of their heads.

That's when the out-of-body thing started. After that, it was like I was watching myself. I went back to the door, crouched as low as I could and inched back out into the hallway. I could see Mike looking in carefully and I motioned to him that there were two deceased in the room I had just left. I didn't have a hand gesture to indicate they were kids or that I was operating on autopilot.

I made for the next door down the hallway. It was a bathroom. There was an adult female dead in the bath. Blood had flowed down the tile behind her and into the bathwater. Probably the kids' mother. There was a single gunshot wound to her forehead as well.

Mike tried calling out to Juarez.

"Johnny, just put down your weapon and come on out of there," he said.

The reply was two more shots, one hitting about the same spot on the wall where the other shots had gone, the other out the open door and across the parking lot, shattering the back window of an old Subaru but otherwise causing no harm.

"No, daddy, don't!" came another scream.

I stood up, took about five full speed steps into the apartment's living room, and saw Johnny Juarez sitting in a La-Z-Boy recliner, holding onto his daughter as he tried to put a shot into her head. She was maybe four, but she was strong enough to move her head out of the way as he pulled the trigger. The shot went through the television instead.

That's when Juarez saw me, turned and fired. It hit me like a thunderclap in the ribs on my left side and almost spun me around. He shoved the little girl aside, stood up, leveled the gun at me again, and squeezed the trigger.

Click.

He was out. And I was on him.

I like to say I don't remember what came next, but the truth is that I do have flashes of it from time to time. I don't know all the details, but it's not that hard to piece together a reasonable idea of what happened.

I darted forward, tackling Juarez, taking him backward, and crashing through the sliding glass door that led out to a tiny fenced in patio area. I pounded a strong right down on his nose, then kicked the gun out of his hand with my left leg. It slid across the patio deck and out of his reach.

He tried to throw me off, but I hit him with another right and then brought the butt of my weapon down with my left on his forehead. He made some kind of gasping sound, and then I just repeated a series of rights. His face was a bloody mess of meat when Mike finally struggled with one arm to pull me off him.

The parking lot was a sea of cop cars, lights flashing, radios barking, onlookers gawking. I remember handing Juarez's daughter to someone – everyone said it was Sgt. Sarah Block, but I can't quite see it in my head – and sitting in the back of an ambulance as they checked me out.

My right hand was broken, but I couldn't feel it until later at the hospital when I was getting checked out. At about the same time my ribs really started to let me know they weren't happy with the day's events. But hurt ribs were way, way better than it would have been without the vest.

* * *

I was released about four hours later. Mike spent the night in the hospital, but was released the next day. Given the situation and following the normal protocols, I was put on administrative leave and I accepted the department's offer of counseling.

After about eight weeks, I was cleared of any wrong-doing and two weeks after that I was officially reinstated.

That was my last day on the force. I turned in my badge and my weapon and had no idea what I was going to do.

Just not *that* ever again.

CHAPTER 2

TUESDAY

I placed a call to Sgt. Nick Molsby at the Hurst Police Department. The officer who answered the phone told me that Nick was in a meeting and would be glad to return my call if I cared to leave a message. Having known him for many years, I didn't really recall him ever being glad to return calls. But maybe she knew him better.

I left my name and number with her and she thanked me for calling. I'm not one to point fingers at folks for having too much morning caffeine, but she should consider switching to decaf.

I got back to work and finished writing down the details of my conversation with Mrs. Jean Hollander. Everyone has their own way of doing things. My approach was to first notate the facts, then go back through and describe her opinions and then my initial questions about both the facts and her opinions. Sometimes seeing something written down and clearly indicated as opinion helped me to dismiss it and go back to the facts.

As if to compensate for me being a half hour early, Michelle Benson, my partner, came in a half hour late, cursing in words that weren't understandable and almost visibly followed by one of those personal cartoon rain clouds.

I looked up from my notes as Michelle threw her purse at her desk chair. It skidded across her desk, sent the papers that had been piled there flying, slid off the desk into the back of her chair, knocking the chair over backward into the plant of indeterminate lineage she had been trying to nurture for the past three months. It, in turn, tipped over and spilled dirt from the pot in which it was planted.

"Morning, Michelle," I said and started making notes again as if this happened every day – it didn't – and did my best just to wait for her to tell me whatever was bothering her.

"Shut-up, Donovan!" she said. "I don't want to hear from any man – even you – today, so just keep your mouth shut and don't talk to me."

"We've got a case," I said.

"Damn," she said. She hung up her jacket and began cleaning up the mess she had just made. I finished my notes, turned the page and started doodling so it would look like I wasn't watching her. She was cute even when she was angry.

She was a 5'2" blonde with a lot of energy and a fair amount of attitude, as her entrance today suggested, and she was also a pretty decent shot on the target range. She was also the organizational one in our office, so it didn't take her very long to have things put right. As she finished, I decided to offer a guess to speed the process along.

"Did he forget to tell you he was married?"

"He forgot to tell me he was a jerk."

"Seems like that would be a hard thing to forget, at least

on the surface of it," I said. "Unlike, say, being an idiot, which sort of implies that one might forget that…"

"I said not to talk to me."

"Yeah, but I wasn't listening," I said.

"Probably true," she said.

She worked quickly and efficiently. She kept things where they were supposed to be and she had a logical reason for the order in which they were filed. In addition to her organizational genius, she was also a first rate, licensed private investigator on her own. While it was technically my agency and while I did most of the field work, she's my partner. Even on days like this one.

I carefully tore the pages from my notepad along their perforated edges and handed them to Michelle. She started reading them right away as the phone rang.

"Donovan Bay Investigations," I said.

"Molsby," Molsby said.

"You don't sound glad to be calling me back."

"It isn't enough that I sent a client to you? Now I have to be happy that you're going to hit me up for inside information you shouldn't have?"

"A fair question. Can I at least buy you lunch?"

"You're not just buying me lunch. You're buying me a good lunch. No Taco Bueno," he said.

His implication was true. Taco Bueno was my default setting.

"Where and when?" I asked.

"Sutherland's. Noon."

No good-bye. He hung up, so I hung up. Michelle finished

reading the notes.

"I know this case," she said. "Doesn't seem like there's much there, except a set of parents who want to know why their son was killed, which is pretty reasonable. What did Molsby have to say?"

"Nothing yet. I'm buying him lunch at Sutherland's."

"You usually take me to Taco Bueno," she said. "But that's okay. I like Taco Bueno." Yet another reason she was my partner.

"Who's the detective on the case?"

"That's one of the things that wasn't in the file Mrs. Hollander gave me."

"She gave you a file and you gave it to me when…?"

I reached for the file on top of my desk and handed it to her.

"If we're going to do our own investigation from the ground up on this one, we better get started," she said.

"I'm going to go check out some locations before lunch," I said and headed toward the door.

"Any hunches?" Michelle asked.

"Not a one," I said without looking back.

CHAPTER 3

I decided to run by the victim's place of work, as well as his residence and his parents' home, all three of which he had visited in the hours preceding his death. I didn't plan on getting access to any of them yet; I just wanted to get a feel for things. I got in my car, started it up, backed out of my spot and headed out.

* * *

It had been a cool, crisp morning with the sun shining in a bright blue sky and an early, distinct hint of fall in the air. Since it was early in the day and some of them were just arriving as well, the building's other tenants greeted me with waves, head nods, howdies or hellos as I walked along the first floor's sidewalk and headed up the stairs to my office.

I'm not a morning person normally – if ever – but the sunshine had been hard to ignore, chiefly because I had forgotten to close my blinds the night before and the effort of getting up to close them had sufficiently awakened me to the point that trying to go back to sleep for an extra 20 or 30 minutes would have been pointless.

I had been out late with the instructor and a couple of the other students from a cooking class I had taken on a whim. I had always loved food. Now I *loved* it. I pretty much hated self-describing with any adjective that ended in "ie" but I had, in fact, become a foodie. The chance to hang out with Chef Lauren was not to be passed up, no matter what sleep was sacrificed.

So, coffee in hand, I trotted up the stairs to the second floor and found someone standing outside my office.

The someone was Mrs. Jean Hollander, she said. She was a nice-looking woman, in maybe her early 60s but could pretty easily pass for early 50s. Dark black hair, done simply but elegantly. Light on the make-up. On the well-dressed side of business casual. I suspected "business" meant "housewife," but that was just a first impression. I trusted my gut instinct most of the time, but never carved its edicts in stone.

She also looked as if she had been carrying a lot of weight of the emotional variety for some time. She seemed to be doing so with some degree of grace.

I opened the door, reached in, clicked on the lights – unnecessary with the daylight pouring in through the big front window – and motioned her in ahead of me. I followed.

"I'm sorry to come so early," she said. "I just got here and didn't want to go back home and then come back."

"It's no problem," I said.

The coffee maker had already completed its daily duties and I offered her a cup. She declined and took a seat in front of my desk, her back to the front window. I hung my Rangers jacket over the back of my chair and sat down facing her. Dust swirled in the bright, angled rays of the morning light. The ceiling fan hummed overhead as the ceiling fan started and then wooshed away almost immediately as it got up to speed. No air conditioner this morning, maybe not until the afternoon sun hit full force and maybe not even then. A nice break.

But Mrs. Jean Hollander didn't come to talk about the weather.

"Sgt. Molsby with the Hurst Police Department gave me your name when I asked if they could recommend a good private investigator," she said. "It's about my son."

I pulled a notepad and a pen from the center drawer of my desk and started writing.

"Okay, Mrs. Hollander. I appreciate Sgt. Molsby referring you. What can you tell me about your son and what it is that brings you to me?"

She reached into her purse and pulled out a green file folder that had been protruding from it. She spoke very calmly.

"My son, Roger, was murdered last year, and I think the police are giving up on the case."

She handed the folder to me. I set down my pen and opened it. Inside, stapled to one side, was a color photo of a handsome young man along with a series of photocopies of newspaper clippings on the other. She was still talking, but she didn't need to. I knew the case. Everyone in the Dallas/Forth Worth Metroplex knew the case.

"Of course I heard about this when it happened, Mrs. Hollander, and I'm very sorry for your loss. I'll be happy to talk with you about this case, but I want you to know that the Hurst Police Department hasn't given up on it. I know them well enough to say that without even talking to them."

"Officially they haven't given up and they won't," she said. "I know that. But look at the statistics. They have less than a murder a year. They have what I'm told is called a very good 'closure rate.' They're just not set up for a case that goes on and on like this. Most small towns aren't."

When I'm talking to a client, prospective client or witness, I try to keep my facial and other body language reactions to a minimum. They tend to interfere with what the person is trying to tell me, and sometimes what they're trying not to tell me. I must have raised an eyebrow or something because she stopped and smiled a sad, genuine smile.

"In the last year, I've learned all the jargon. I might not get the terms right, but I understand their meaning. Our police department isn't set up for a murder investigation that goes on this long," she said.

"Fair enough," I said, "but Hurst isn't exactly a small town."

"And it's not exactly Dallas or Ft. Worth or Arlington either," she said.

The statistics were what the statistics were, so I didn't protest further. It would be easy enough to argue either way. HPD's closure rate on murders was nearly 100% over a very long stretch. On the other hand, the longer the crime went unsolved the greater the likelihood it would stay that way. There are plenty of unsolved crimes in any town this size.

I offered her some coffee again and she declined again, and she told me about the case.

Her son, who had worked in the family business as a

young boy, started his own company as a teenager, and become a prominent, prosperous member of the community had been found dead in his store, stabbed so many times that the Tarrant County Medical Examiner's office had actually brought in an outside consultant to help them correctly identify the number of wounds.

Fourteen months, two weeks and three days later there were officially still no suspects. I looked Mrs. Jean Hollander in the eyes and took the case.

CHAPTER 4

It hadn't taken long for Mrs. Hollander to lay out what she had. What she said clocked well against what I already knew. The *Fort Worth Star-Telegram* and the *Dallas Morning News* had covered most of the salient points that the local TV news had glossed over or simply got wrong. HPD had undoubtedly held some details back.

I asked her to tell me about her son.

"I know the police have asked you these sorts of things over and over, and I'm sorry to put you through it again," I said.

"I'm glad to do it if it brings us any closer to catching whoever did this," she said.

Roger Crowder Hollander was 42 years old when he was killed. The oldest of three children – his sisters were 12 and 10 years younger, respectively, and both now lived out of state – he had graduated from L.D Bell High School in Bedford, the University of North Texas in Denton, and had completed a law degree at Southern Methodist University in Dallas, although he never sat for the Bar Exam or practiced law.

He had played football and baseball at Bell and football at

UNT. A knee injury there had ended his playing days. He had done some volunteer coaching at SMU, but had given that up when he decided his true calling was business, she said.

His father, Steven Drake Hollander, now retired, had been a civically active owner of a pair of prominent automobile dealerships, one Ford and one Honda, in Hurst and a Chrysler dealership in Euless, which was two towns over. My brother had played baseball on a team sponsored by the Ford dealership in a championship game against the team sponsored by the Honda dealership. That had made at least one of the TV stations' sportscasts back when.

The elder Hollander had been a board member for two local hospitals as well as numerous charitable institutions and civic organizations. He had been followed by his son, who had worked in the family business throughout junior high school and early in high school.

Late in high school, though, Roger had asked his father to stake him in opening a cellular phone kiosk at the mall. Staffing the kiosk first with himself and friends and then others, he had ridden the explosion of cellular service. The kiosk became a store, the store became several stores, and so on.

"Good thing he got into law school on a scholarship," Mrs. Hollander smiled wistfully. "If I had paid for that degree and he didn't use it, I would have brained him. But his father loved the fact that he knew what his calling was. Said it was the same way with him."

Obvious questions: Did he have any enemies? Was he in a relationship or had he been recently? Was there any area or detail in particular that she believed that HPD had overlooked or dismissed too quickly?

No, no, and no.

None of this was too surprising. Even if someone believes he or she has an enemy or enemies, their families rarely know about it unless some physical altercation has already happened. And once they left home – and frequently beforehand – young adults didn't tend to talk that much about relationships that weren't permanent. The fact that Mrs. Hollander didn't know about any negatives didn't mean there weren't any, just that she didn't know about them.

"What kind of a kid was he?" I asked.

"Good. A bit driven. I always wished that he could have a little less of that and his sisters a little more, but we had a good bit of money by the time they were teenagers… Anyway, Roger always went after what he wanted. It's how he succeeded. After my husband loaned him the money to start the business, I don't think he ever borrowed another cent."

"Really?"

"Oh, I'm sure Steve co-signed for some loans or called in some favors when Roger expanded his operations, but he paid his own way and paid back all the money he originally borrowed from us," she said.

"Well, as a small business owner myself, that's pretty impressive," I said.

Mrs. Hollander smiled. She nodded and the smile wavered when I told her I wanted to ask about the evening of the murder. She told me that she didn't know anything more than what she had said to the police.

Roger had worked at his mall store that day, training a

new assistant manager. He had stopped by his parents' house in Bedford to deliver a new phone to his mother, and then left to work in his warehouse. He kept a sort of apartment on the warehouse's second floor. That's where he was killed. No one had missed him until the next morning when he was discovered by a manager from one of his stores who had arrived to pick up some new inventory. He had been found in the living room, stabbed repeatedly in the chest. The manager had called 911, but Roger was pronounced dead at the scene. The autopsy was able to determine that he had been that way for several hours.

I thanked her for going over it with me. This was not the kind of child's death a parent ever makes their peace with, regardless of how old that child was. She handled it well, better than I thought I would have if the roles were reversed.

She wrote me a check to cover the first week and I told her I'd get started right away.

"I don't have any illusions about this. You may not be able to do anything more than the police," she said, "but unlike them, this will be your job. While we are paying you, I expect this to be your primary focus."

If she had seen my bank account, she would have known that her case had my undivided attention.

CHAPTER 5

"About time you showed up," Molsby said.

"I'm right on time," I replied. It was always a mistake to back down to Nick Molsby, particularly when you had to ask him for something.

"I've been hungry for a half hour."

"I'll send you the name of the new energy bars Michelle has been trying. She swears by 'em."

With a small wave of two fingers, I simultaneously caught the hostess's attention and let her know that we'd need a table for two. She smiled, finished seating a nice looking older couple, and came over to where we were standing. She picked up two menus and asked us to follow her.

I would have said "Anywhere," but it would only have been to irritate Molsby and I only wanted to do that after I had what I needed from him.

She showed us to a table. We sat down and she handed us our menus.

"Tommy will be your server today and he'll be right with you," she said, then turned and went back to the entryway to greet the latest arrivals. It was the lunch hour, and we knew from experience that Sutherland's would fill up quickly.

"Great," said Molsby. "A dude waitress. I would have preferred a waitress-waitress."

Sometimes I didn't know whether he was being serious or not. And sometimes, even after knowing him all those years, I actually made the mistake of asking. But not today. I just glanced over my menu and him and quietly shook my head, then went back to trying to pick out what I was having for lunch.

There were a number of good things from which to choose. The noise level also didn't hurt. It wouldn't be so loud that we would have to shout, but it would be enough that we could have a conversation with a reasonable expectation that others wouldn't be able to hear us.

Tommy came and took our orders. Molsby had an unsweetened ice tea and the pulled pork sandwich. I asked for the same thing. Tommy thanked us and went off to turn in our order.

"Bet he messes it up," Molsby said.

"What made you send Mrs. Hollander to me?"

"She asked for a good P.I. Didn't think you'd object."

"You know what I mean, Nick. What brought the investigation to the point it seemed like the prudent course of action for you, a Hurst Police Sergeant, to recommend to the mother of a murder victim, that she should seek the assistance of outside help, namely me?"

"Investigation's not going anywhere. No new leads for months. Never any really good ones to start with," he said.

"Sounds promising," I said.

"There's been a seven percent jump in burglaries on the south side of 183 in the last quarter. Squeaky wheel. Grease. All that."

"So while the file will stay active, it's not going to be active-active? Sad, but probably realistic. What's your take?"

"Wasn't very involved in the case originally, but after this long almost everyone's been into it in some way or another," he said. "Just got to know the victim's mother, Mrs. Hollander, and like her enough to want her to have some peace of mind."

Tommy arrived with our orders on a tray. He set down Molsby's ice tea and then mine, his sandwich and then mine.

"Will there be anything else?" he asked with a smile.

"The sandwiches," Molsby growled. "Pulled pork?"

"Uh, yes, sir," Tommy said.

"Why'd he get onion rings and I get fries with it then?"

No missing it – though I had chosen not to say anything – the big galoot was right.

Whatever a galoot was.

Tommy stammered a bit: "Well, sir, I, uh, that is…"

"Just say it's a mistake, Tommy," I said.

"Sorry, sir, it's a mistake. I can go switch it out…" Tommy said.

"No need, Tommy," I said. I asked Molsby if he liked onion rings, and he did. I gave him my plate and took his. I was fine either way. Tommy apologized again and went on his way after promising to come back and check on us.

"Dude waitresses, man. I tell you what," Molsby said and shook his head.

"Who's the lead detective on the case?" I changed the

subject.

"Ginger Baker," he said as he bit into his sandwich.

"Ginger Baker, the late drummer of 1960s power trio Cream as well as Blind Faith?" I asked and bit into my own sandwich. It was really good, and the idea that the lead detective on the case had played with Eric Clapton appealed to me. Even if he was technically deceased.

"Ginger Baker, as in the young but pretty good detective who's been with the force three years. Used to be out at DFW and did a year in Dallas, too."

"Why the moves?" I asked. No Eric Clapton. I tried not to be depressed.

"Finding her place. Good cop. Grew up around here. Went to L.D. Bell."

L.D. Bell High School, my alma matter. Yay.

We finished our meal. True to his word, Tommy had checked on our progress a couple more times. As I was paying the tab, Molsby slid a napkin across the table to me. I took and slid it the rest of the way across the table. There was a memory stick underneath it, and it fell into my lap as I picked up the napkin and wiped my mouth with it.

"Thanks," I said.

I pocketed the memory stick and pulled out my car keys.

"We'll have to do this again soon," I said.

"But probably Taco Bueno," he said.

"Probably," I said.

Molsby would have gotten in trouble for just giving me a copy of the entire case file. He trusted that I knew not to trip up or to cross the line in using the material. I had more than proven myself over the years. His superiors would almost definitely have given me a look at the file, but that would have been it. This was a major head start.

I headed back to the office. I was there in less than 10 minutes. I tried not to take the steps two at a time, but in that I failed. I wanted to see what was in the file on the murder of Roger Hollander.

When I did, my brain started to explode.

CHAPTER 6

The first thing I did after I plugged the memory stick Nick Molsby had given me into the USB port on my computer, even before I opened the files up and looked at them, was to copy the contents to off-site storage. I don't want to sound like an advertisement for backing up your files, but I've had everything from lost term papers in college to someone breaking into my office before, so I learned it the hard way and now I'm almost obsessive about it.

Before this, I'd only seen the couple of standard photos of Roger Hollander that the press had run. Not including the crime scene pictures, there were several different images of the deceased.

Suddenly something clicked, at least partially. I knew this guy, if only I could remember how. He was four years older than me, so we didn't go to high school together and we weren't at UNT at the same time...

I knew it would come to me if I left it alone, so I did. I moved onto the witness statement of the employee who had found him. There wasn't a lot beyond what Mrs. Hollander had told me, but I would have Michelle read over it and compare it to the notes I had taken. To me it looked like all the important stuff was there. Then there were the crime scene photos, almost two hundred of them. First I looked at the ones that had been flagged.

The shots that were overviews of the crime scene showed the placement around the room, what was where, and so on. They also gave someone looking at things after the fact, someone like me, the ability to understand the context of the more detailed, close-up shots.

The first thing that stood out, even in a still photograph – it occurred to me that there was probably video in these files, too – was the viciousness of the attack on Roger Hollander. In comparison to other crime scene photos, you could tell something was just off. The violence wasn't directed against the room but almost solely against him. There would be more of this in the closer shots, so I tried to concentrate on other details around the room. There was an open bottle of wine on the coffee table. There were a number of magazines on it as well, as was an open book with black and white photographs. Nothing really jumped out about them. Same with most of the rest of the room. I printed the crime scene report so I could look at it and the photos without jumping back and forth between windows.

There was a significant amount of blood splattered around the immediate area, with some reaching as far as the bookcases that lined the far wall, the bar that occupied much of the wall to the right, and the glass on the large window to the left. There would no doubt be photos of the blood splatter patterns. Experts could tell a lot from it and computer models were becoming even more sophisticated than they had been just a couple of years earlier. They could tell a lot from the crime just by using their advanced math.

No one was going to need much to see the brutality of this particular crime. In just a medium shot, not even a close-up, a lot more was evident. He wasn't just dead. Most of the physical shape of his chest – presuming it had been normal previously – had been eviscerated by the multiple stab wounds. I was pretty sure I didn't want to look at the close-ups, but I did so anyway. Forming a hypothesis at this point in an investigation often led to spending lots of time working to support that theory. In this case, though, it was hard not to jump to conclusions while looking at the photos of the victim. There was just so much… rage. The little voice inside my head, my gut, whatever you wanted to call it, said this was not some crazy loner or burglary gone bad or drug deal or anything like that. This was personal. So even if Mrs. Hollander didn't think her son had any enemies, the evidence in front of me seemed to beg to differ.

There wasn't going to be any putting this idea entirely out of my head, so I wrote it down on my notepad with a big question mark. I stared at the photos again for a few minutes, then slid my chair back from my desk and walked over to get a drink of water. I drank it, threw the cup away, went outside and sat down on the stairs that led up to our floor.

I looked around and tried to think about anything else. You have to take a clinical approach with scenes like the one at which I'd been looking, but I wasn't one of those people who could really do it. I mean, sure, I could muscle through the muck and get the job done, but I didn't really ever want to get to the point where that stuff didn't bother me. Something like that *should* bother you, I figured. If it didn't, you had issues, and if you pretended it didn't, you had other issues.

Michelle came out and handed me a cold Dr. Pepper. She shrugged, which was her way of saying she didn't know what to say, then she turned around and went back inside. I popped the top, heard the fizz, took a sip, and stared blankly at the traffic for a few minutes. I watched the cars and trucks go by and people – not many of them – coming and going on the parking lot below. I stared at my shoes and the concrete on the stairs for a few minutes, too, but there wasn't any avoiding it. The only thing to do was to get back to work.

The pictures wouldn't leave my mind. Neither would my first instinct. Roger Hollander knew his killer.

CHAPTER 7

After another hour of looking at the crime scene photos, reports, and assorted related documents, I decided that I didn't want to be a private investigator anymore. I wanted a job that involved watching cartoons and spending perhaps an hour or two a day at the batting cages. Instead of going with these instincts, I decided to go check out several of Roger Hollander's business locations.

I needed to simultaneously clear my head and keep working on the case, so taking a short drive seemed as likely as anything else to help me. Taking things for granted leads to a lot of mistakes, but we have to make certain assumptions in order to be able to function in our daily lives.

Without knowing the officer on the case, there were some pretty basic steps that it was reasonable to take as given:

They had investigated every angle they thought of.

They had talked to everyone they thought to talk to.

They had come up with every possible motive that seemed reasonable.

And by process of elimination they had ruled out all of the scenarios, potential suspects and motives until only the frustrating, bare bones facts remained. The most brutal murder that anyone on the Hurst Police Department could remember simply lingered on.

What that meant was that to get any further than the police had, I would have to see something they didn't, find a mistake they had made, or get lucky. Any or all of the options were long shots, but that didn't mean one or more of them couldn't happen. Whatever the outcome, it would require a lot of work. We'd be going back over as much as possible of the same ground the police had already covered, challenging their assumptions and our own, and hoping that we looked at something differently enough to let us figure out how the pieces of the puzzle fit together.

In other words, like anything worthwhile, it was going to be a lot of work.

Northeast Mall, site of the victim's biggest store, was a monument to eminent domain. No question, it was a financial benefit to the community, but the idea that government could seize a property from its rightful owners and then turn around and sell it to a for-profit enterprise was not the same thing as taking the property to build a highway or school. It was done a few more years back than I cared to remember, but it still irritated me. The phrase "Get over it." was never very high on my list.

I entered near the food court – the mall's only substandard feature – and walked past the legions of pre-teens, teens, and proto-teens gathered there. A few individual adults and families dotted the tables, but school must have been out because there were kids everywhere. Everyone was on their cell phones.

As I left the food court area, a quick left and then not too far later a right brought me to Roger Hollander's biggest and most successful store. A franchise from one of the larger cell phone service providers, it was a basic, attractively designed, straight forward looking business. I looked at it for a few moments. Nothing out of the ordinary, or so it seemed, and then I went in.

All of the employees were clad in uniform white shirts with red trim and khaki slacks. I was greeted by a bubbly brunette whose name tag said "Bunny" and who was trying too hard. When I asked to see the manager, she turned down her bubbliness by about 50 percent and pointed toward a tall, broad fellow on the other side of the store. She said his name was Larry Green. He looked like a jerk, but I tried to keep an open mind.

When I introduced myself and told him I was looking into the case at the request of Hollander's parents, he stuck out his hand and tried to do one of those Al Gore crush-your-hand moves that jerks always do. A firm handshake remains one measure of a man. Macho bullshit remains the measure of a man who doesn't measure up in other areas.

Rule to remember: There's always someone stupid around the next corner.

I met his grip with equal intensity. He had size and weight on me, so I made a face at him like he was an idiot. That surprised him and took him out of his game for a moment.

"Perhaps you didn't hear me correctly," I said as calmly as possible. "I am working for your late boss's parents."

He relaxed his grip. I did as well.

"Oh, uh, I didn't realize you worked for the Hollanders," he mumbled. "We should go into my office."

He turned and walked ahead of me. He opened the door to the back area of the store and I followed him through. I waited for him to do something else stupid, but he didn't. He sat down behind a desk and motioned for me to sit down opposite him. I did.

"What can I tell you about Roger?" he asked, suddenly cooperative and eager to avoid eye contact.

"What was he like to work for? What did employees think of him?"

"He was an okay boss. He didn't interact with the regular employees a whole lot because he was at the main office and they were at the stores, but I think most of the managers on the other shifts or at the other stores would say the same thing. I wouldn't have stuck around for five years if he wasn't a good boss, ya know?" he said.

He looked up at that point, wanting to see if I liked what I was hearing. I kept my expression as neutral as possible.

"So he didn't come around to the stores very much?"

"Oh, he visited each of the stores at least once a week. It's just that as long as things were going well, he didn't actually work in them or hang out for very long, ya know?"

I nodded yes.

"Okay. Who interacted with him the most?"

"In our store that would be Marco Longoria, our dayshift manager. The daytime managers and assistant managers were the ones who worked with Roger the most because they would go to meetings and pick up products at the main office, ya know?"

I nodded again.

"Now I'm sure the police asked this question back when the incident took place, but can you think of anyone who'd want to hurt Mr. Hollander?"

"Yeah, they asked that. They asked that question about a dozen different ways, but I couldn't even think of anyone who had anything bad to say about him. Even the people who get fired here, it's usually me or Marco that fires 'em, so I don't know what they'd have against Roger," he said.

"Okay, one last question," I said. I waited until he brought his gaze up again and made strong eye contact with him. "When I came in here, it was clear that you weren't too happy about me asking about Mr. Hollander's death. Why was that?"

"Uh, I just didn't know why you were here. How he died was gruesome and I don't really like talking about it," Larry said. "Sorry."

It was a feeble excuse. I reached in my pocket and pulled out one of my cards. I handed it to him.

"Here's my card. If you think of anything else, give me a call."

He said he would. I didn't believe him, but why let him know that?

CHAPTER 8

It was getting near dinner time, which meant I wasn't about to head toward Roger Hollander's next closest store at Southlake Town Square until after rush hour died down. I figured it would clear up – as much as it was going to – around 7 PM, so I decided to grab some dinner and then figure another way to kill some time first.

I called Michelle and asked if she wanted to join me. She had plans that included a long, hot bath, a big glass of wine, and turning off her cell phone unless I really, really thought I'd need her for anything. I told her I really, really didn't expect to, for which she thanked me by saying "Good" and hanging up.

Starting my car and dropping it into gear, I pulled out of the parking space and headed for the nearest Taco Bueno, which was the one across from L.D. Bell High School. I had a Dr. Pepper, two tacos, a beef burrito, and several doses of taco sauce sitting in front of me. The drive-through was hopping, but inside just a few other customers occupied the dining area. If they had been playing music from my playlist, it would have been perfect.

I didn't know anymore about the case than I did when

I left the office, except that Larry Green at Hollander's Northeast Mall store was a jerk and that he, in turn, thought Hollander had been good to work for. Nothing to do but keep nosing around. I flashed back on some of the documents and photos I had looked at. I really tried to not concentrate on the photos while I was eating, but there was something about one of them. I didn't know what it was. I let it go and savored the burrito. Not that I'd let anyone know, but I had been trying to eat a lot healthier lately. Luckily, I actually liked salads and soups. So, this really was a treat. And it never got old.

I thought about Hollander. Not just the victim, but the guy. How the heck did I know this guy? He was four years ahead of me in school. His sisters were six and eight years behind me, respectively, so I didn't go to school with any of them. My brother was three years younger than me, so he didn't either. Everyone knew his family's name. I was beginning to convince myself that it was just between the car dealerships and my brother playing on a ball team they sponsored. But something floated just out of reach.

I finished my dinner, dumped the trash in the trashcan and put the tray on top of the can where others were stacked. I put more ice in my cup, refilled the Dr. Pepper, and wrapped a napkin around the cup, checked my watch and headed for my car. There was still time to kill before I'd want to hit the road to Southlake. It was a Tuesday, so the Hurst Public Library was open until 9 p.m., and that would help.

Laura Field was working the front desk at the library. I could have called and found that out ahead of time, but I had been headed there anyway. She smiled when she saw me. She put a couple of books on the top shelf of a cart and then came out from behind the counter and gave me a big hug.

She was 5'6" with short, spikey blonde, pink and purple hair. She looked great, had a super smile and a penchant for 1980s music. And as hot as she was to look at, her mind was probably sexier. She was a Brainiac of the first order and loved researching things. In terms of book smarts, she lived on a level I rarely – if ever – visited. As an investigator, I'd take my situational experience over the theoretical stuff every time, but she'd broken more than a few detail-oriented cases for me. And when you got down to it, they were all detail-oriented.

We had survived dating in high school, survived her coming out, and survived those moments when I awkwardly thought there might still be some spark between us. And we were actually still good friends.

"What's up, Donovan? Working?" She slipped her arm around mine.

"Yeah. Remember the Hollander murder last year?"

"Oh, of course. I think he dated my cousin back in high school or something. I didn't know him at all, but sure, I remember the case," she said. "What do you need?"

I looked around. I didn't see anyone else there.

"We have the place to ourselves?" I asked. "I have some of the newspaper articles from around the time of the murder, but they don't tell me anything."

"Bunch of kids doing some school project, some other folks, but it's pretty quiet. I should be able to start while I'm here and do some more from home. You need it tonight?"

"Not tonight," I said. "We just got started with it. As soon as you can, but don't put yourself out for it."

She turned and looked at me, tilting her head. "This is where I make a joke about putting out, right?"

"You're just cruel."

"Not just. I'll probably give you a call tomorrow evening," she said.

I thanked her, gave her another hug, and turned toward the door. As I did, I saw a set of yearbooks from L.D. Bell on the shelf.

"What's the story there?" I nodded to them.

"Both Bell and Trinity donated full sets to the libraries in Hurst, Euless and Bedford. We just got them," she said. "They go all the way back."

I walked up and pulled out the year I graduated. I looked at it, flipped through, looking for a specific image. I stopped when I found it.

"What is it, Donovan?" she said from behind me. I set the book down on the counter at an angle, then adjusted it slightly to match what I remembered. Then I stepped about 15 feet away to approximate the view.

"It's been bugging me since I saw the crime scene photos. I couldn't remember it, but now I do. I worked on the yearbook when I went to Bell," I said. "There was a copy of this one at the murder site and I want to know why."

CHAPTER 9

Jennifer O'Connor answered the phone on the second ring.

"Digs, it's me. What're you doing?" I said.

It was getting darker and I was driving from the Hurst Public Library to Hollander's store at Southlake Town Square. Night was beginning to arrive and the air was pleasant. I pushed the button on my door and the window rose up to cut down on the background noise.

"Just getting ready for bed. I have an obscenely early phone conference tomorrow," she said.

"Listen to you, all responsible and so forth."

"I know. It's totally lame being a grown up, isn't it? Not all that many years ago I'd just be getting ready to go out about now. What's going on?"

"Working on a case. Trying to figure out something about a vague high school memory that I can't quite put together. I figured maybe you could help me with it since you knew everyone who was anyone and most of the rest of us, too," I said.

"I'm actually free tomorrow night. Want to grab dinner? I ought to be home pretty early, like by 5 o'clock or so," she said.

"Sounds great. I'll see you then," I said. She was silent for just a moment.

"It's good to hear your voice, Donovan. No one ever calls me Digs anymore," she said.

"Their loss, Digs. And as nice as it is to hear you, it'll be even better to see you," I said. We said our goodnights and hung up.

To anyone eavesdropping, it certainly wouldn't have sounded like anything out of the ordinary. I thought about it, though, and decided it had been five years since we had last talked. And as normal as the short dialogue would have sounded to anyone else, to me the words echoed with resounding sentiment. I laughed out loud as I drove along Grapevine Highway, also known as Highway 26. I couldn't stop smiling.

The rush hour traffic had indeed subsided. Nothing was like those semi-mythical "good old days" when you could get anywhere in the Metroplex in a short time, but such was progress. I headed down Grapevine Highway to Brumlow, which then turns into Carroll Avenue and takes you right into Southlake Town Center.

Like a lot of open air malls that had popped up around the country in the last two decades, it was one that tried to re-create the small town squares that we as a society had torn down decades earlier so we could replace them with enclosed monstrosities. Texas actually had many remaining actual town squares, which were usually centered around fantastic, old county courthouses. There wasn't a lot of money in pointing out the obvious, though, so they built these new ones and people came here to shop and eat.

From the outside, Hollander's store looked like many of the other establishments there: nice, clean, safe, and even inviting. They didn't have a lot of individuality or unique characteristics, but walking around on the sidewalks outside the various shops was an enjoyable experience, which is exactly the purpose for which it was designed.

Once inside, the store mostly resembled the one at Northeast Mall and, I suspected, the rest of them. I was greeted by a young lady made from the same mold as the one that greeted me at the Northeast Mall store. When I asked her for the manager, she pointed me to Kayla Singh, who was standing on the other side of the store and just finishing up with another customer.

As soon as the other customer departed, I walked up and introduced myself to Ms. Singh. She was strikingly pretty, dressed in their requisite uniform, yet somehow she managed to make it look not just cute but sexy. I told her that Hollander's parents had hired me and that I'd be going over at least some of the same ground as the police. Her face was a study in professional cooperativeness and personal ambivalence. She cared precisely as much as it related to her paycheck to do so.

She showed me into her office. Like the interior layout of the sales area and the uniforms, it was very similar to the other one I'd been to earlier. Maybe the photocopier was different. I don't know.

"What can I do to help you, Mr. Bay?" she said as she sat down at her desk. She motioned for me to take the chair in front of it, which I did.

"I'm just trying to get a feel for how things worked with Mr. Hollander's business. Was he in the store very often?"

"I don't know what you might mean by often, but he was here once a week most weeks, same as our other stores in the region. He had other regional managers who covered similar size areas in San Antonio and Austin, but he covered our home office region in that capacity himself," she said. She had a beautiful, distinct voice. I surmised she would probably be very difficult to negotiate with. She had been with the company for four years and was being considered to run the region that Hollander had covered. Hollander's father, who had come on board as a caretaker CEO, had no interest in that particular aspect of the job.

Her observations of the business were very similar to those Larry Green had expressed, though her regard for Roger Hollander seemed a bit forced. I couldn't tell whether she just didn't care or didn't want to speak ill of the dead.

"From talking to one of the guys over the Northeast Mall store, I got the idea that Roger Hollander was a bit of a jerk," I said. It certainly surprised her. It surprised me, too, since no one had said anything remotely like that to me.

She started to say something. Just enough that her mouth came open for a nanosecond. She recovered quickly, but it had happened.

"I find that difficult to believe since Larry Green was the manager you spoke with, and Larry's nose was about as far up Roger's rear end as it could possibly get," she said.

"Oh, I talked to Larry, too," I said. She was good, but she didn't play poker with Molsby and his colleagues. I did, and my wallet usually lived to tell the tale.

"Please, I should have made this clear before," I offered in a reassuring voice. "Even though I'm working for his parents, I'm not here to report on how employees feel or felt about his management style. I'm just trying to get a feel for things, a real picture of who he was at work, outside of work, and so on. I just want to help them get some peace about this horrible crime."

"I don't really have anything more I want to say about it," she said.

In for a penny, in for a pound, I thought. "Look, we both know that just because he managed men – and particularly brownnosers like Larry Green – one way and women another, doesn't mean that he deserved be brutally murdered. I just thought that being an attractive – and more importantly, intelligent – woman in his company you might have observed something that might help me think about this case differently than all the articles I've read in the newspapers," I said.

Of course I didn't know any such thing about Roger Hollander, and here I was besmirching his good name at his own company.

She started to say something, then she stopped for a moment. Then she started talking in earnest. Then she said a lot.

CHAPTER 10

Sometimes you will hear amazing things if you only just listen.

Kayla Singh was the daughter of Sikh father and a Muslim mother. Receiving discouragement from his parents and a more strident disapproval from hers, they moved to America to seek their fortunes and their own path. They settled first in the borough of Queens in New York City, before a job brought them to Texas. Now both of her parents were Southern Baptists, though her father still wore the turban of his younger days.

When they moved in the late 1970s, they had been the only Indian people on their block or in their town, I would have bet, but they eventually developed real roots in the community. Her father was now a city manager and her mother was an administrator at one of the larger hospitals in the area, and they were co-owners of an Indian restaurant in Grapevine. Kayla had been born and raised in Texas.

Given her distinct voice and speech pattern, this surprised me. I had moved to the Lone Star state as a teenager and had picked up certain verbal affectations by the time I was in my early twenties. I had started using phrases and words like "y'all" as a joke, and soon enough the joke was on me.

When I get really tired, they come out, and not on purpose.

Her grades in high school, she said, had been "stereotypically superb," and she had been involved in everything from AP History to band to the school newspaper. Her parents had given her options when it came to college. She could go to virtually any Ivy League pre-med program followed by medical school and they would pay for everything, including living expenses. Or she could wind up in a cardboard box living in a town park in Euless. I was pretty sure there were more choices than that, but I knew those kind of parents.

She even started at one of the colleges up north before deciding to follow her true passion: jazz. True to their word, her parents had cut her off financially, so she picked up the job working for Roger Hollander to help pay her way through the University of North Texas, where she studied jazz percussion and played in the 1 O'clock Lab Band.

She had a first-generation work ethic and a streak of realism to go with the artsy side, though, so she worked full time in the evenings, banking every cent she could so that when she finished school she could try to make a go of it with jazz and maybe part-time work.

When she started working for Hollander, they had just simultaneously fired two people and added two new spots, so they had four openings. She got one of the spots and enjoyed it because it fit almost perfectly with her school schedule. She said one of the girls that started at the same time as she did developed some sort of relationship with Hollander and soon was the new Assistant Manger.

The woman's name was Lisa Jefferson.

"She still work for the company?" I asked.

"Oh, no. She didn't last eight months," she said. "Please excuse my bluntness, but as soon as Roger was done with her, he was done with her."

I nodded and made a quick note. "I take it you've seen more?"

"I have to say this first. Roger was never unkind, improper or impolite to me. I was never treated poorly in the workplace by him or anyone else," she said. "On the other hand, while it was never said, it was certainly implied that my pay and my advancement would have been better if I had been interested in him outside of work."

"And yet you're a manager and have been for two years."

"Whatever his foibles, Roger was a practical man. I was the best person for the job by far. Combined with Mike McGuckin, who runs the day shift here, I'm part of a team that gives him one less store to worry about. And I suspect he could concentrate on those other stores to find other candidates," she said.

"You think Mr. McGuckin knew about Roger's tendencies?"

"Nope. I don't think most people here even have a clue about this. He was smooth and treated most of the employees fairly, maybe even well if you were to compare our operation to similar ones," she said.

I made a couple more notes, clicked my pen into the closed position, popped it into my pocket and stood up to leave. Kayla got up as well and opened the door for me. She had surprised me in more than one way. I basically liked anyone who did that for starters.

She held out her card to me. She told me that she had written her cell number on the back in case I had anymore questions. I did the same on one of mine and gave it to her. I thanked her again for the information and headed out through the store and into the night life of Southlake Town Square.

Several of the restaurants were still hopping, but most of the traffic appeared to be headed out of the parking lots now and toward the roads leaving the place. I looked at my watch. Too late to go anyplace else, but early enough that Michelle would still be up.

"What?" she answered on the first ring. I kept walking as I headed for my car.

"Met an interesting young Indian woman this evening who told me something other than the Perfect Boy Roger Hollander story," I said.

"I thought I told you to leave me alone this evening," she said.

"Guess I wasn't paying attention."

"Again."

"Sorry."

"Too late for that. Was she hot?"

"Yeah, actually she was."

"Lucky you. So, what did she have to say?"

"Roger wasn't above promoting whomever he was seeing and getting rid of them when he was done," I said.

"Well, that certainly could lead to some animosity. Not

anything taken by itself, but not the most impossible motive I've ever heard," she said.

"Nothing's concrete yet, but this is the first bit that we have that the cops didn't. Might be nothing. Might be something," said.

"You're right. Now leave me alone and let me wallow in my misery."

"You're all cranky," I said.

"I'm taking a bath, Donovan. Leave me alone."

"First tell me what you're wearing right now," I said.

She hung up. I smiled and climbed in my car to head home.

CHAPTER II

It wasn't cold, but there was a hint of crispness in the air. I enjoyed it and kept the windows down. Because it was later and traffic was less, I made it home in about 15 minutes. Just as I put the key in the front door, my cell phone rang. It was Mrs. Hollander.

"I heard you visited a couple of the stores today," she said without any preamble. "If any of them give you any grief or are less than forthcoming, you just call me right away and put me on with them."

Her voice was calm, but certain. The idea of having a new investigator on the case had probably given her a bit of energy, a path out of the no-progress zone. I went into my condo, closed the door behind me, locked it, and flipped the light switch to on.

"That's very kind of you, Mrs. Hollander. I appreciate it. I don't want you to think that I'm onto any big leads or anything yet. I'm just trying to get a feel for things, just starting out. I have a few connections with the police. They've obviously seen their leads dry up, so we're trying to see if there are any ideas they didn't follow up on or any incorrect conclusions that they came to," I said.

I set my keys on my desk and sat myself on my chair.

"You're very diplomatic, Mr. Bay. You're deliberate in your phrasing. You don't want to show up the police and you don't want to get my hopes up in case you don't do any better than they have," she said.

What the heck. When in doubt, tell the truth.

"Yes, ma'am. That's correct."

"Good man. I don't want daily reports unless you're really onto something, in which case I do. I do ask that you check in with me at least weekly, even if there is nothing new. I'm sure you can appreciate my need to at least feel like something is happening."

"I was thinking the same thing as we started talking."

"I am serious, though. If you get anything less than prompt cooperation from any of our people, you let me know."

After promising I would, we hung up. I sat back in the chair and exhaled a long, deliberate stream of air, like a smoker after a long drag. It was a great way to calm one's self, lower the blood pressure a bit, get centered. I closed my eyes and did it again.

I had already cracked one bit of information that the Hurst Police Department hadn't. But a guy who liked to use his influence to date his female employees wasn't exactly the proverbial smoking gun, was it? It might lead nowhere, but we'd have to follow up on it because so far it was just about the only thing we had.

That and the yearbook.

I got up out of the chair and went to my book case. My

yearbooks were on the bottom shelf. I found the one from my senior year and pulled it out, went back to the chair and sat down with it. I flipped through the pages and quickly found the spread I was looking for.

The French club. Okay. Not a major league criminal organization, at least not the year I graduated. I actually heard myself say "Whatever" out loud, which made me laugh. I got up again, set the book on the bar, and grabbed a bottle of Sam Adams from the refrigerator. I popped the top and went back to looking at the pages in the book.

Random memories hit me. I remembered saying "Wait? We have a French Club?" to my fellow yearbook staffers when we got to that section of the book. I knew we had a French Club, of course. Digs had been in the French Club, and my nearly stalker-like devotion in those days required possession of such knowledge. Of course it was about a third the size of the Spanish Club and half again bigger than the German Club, but it was Texas and some things are just to be expected.

I looked at the photo. There were 21 kids standing in three arcing rows of seven, each successive row a little higher than the ones in front of them so all of their faces were visible. Their faculty sponsor, Miss Blackmon, the French teacher, stood to the left side even with the first row. She and most of the kids were smiling. Two girls in the center of the front row each had little French and American flags, their staffs crossed, making an x shape.

Without looking at their names captioned beneath the photo I came up with six of the names in addition to Digs: Rebecca Slater, Jeremy Parkhouse, Gina Gonzales, Becky

Topham, Danny Donaldson, and Roberta... something. Fifth period Algebra. Mrs. Danvers' class. Third seat on the last row. Roberta Whatever.

I cheated: Roberta Tinnell.

Some of the other faces I knew right away, and likewise some of the names in the captions, but I couldn't have put them together. Back then I didn't know how most of them matched up. Outside of Digs and a remarkably small group of friends, I was a social blank in high school. I didn't know Mary Sutherland, David Bradford, Anna Maria Johnson, Louise Haynes, Antonia Kuhoric, Rich Robinson, Ginger Davis or Tommy Daniels. I did recall that Miss Blackmon was pretty hot. She was probably younger then than I was now. Time gives everything perspective.

I copied down the names onto a notepad, then I spent about ten minutes flipping through the book and jotting down which graduating class they were all in. It was pretty evenly split between sophomores, juniors and seniors.

Did it mean anything? Probably not. But why the heck did Roger Hollander have a yearbook from four years after he graduated and why was it open to that page? I didn't even want to think about what the chances were that it would be open to a page I had worked on. Sure, a clue was a clue was a clue, but there was no getting around it: this one was weird. I shook my head as I sat down at my desk. I signed onto my computer and quickly typed up the information in an email to Michelle.

I had pretty much reached my limit for the day. I got ready for bed and I pretended to watch the news for a few minutes while I waited for the weather. I fell asleep before it came on.

CHAPTER 12

WEDNESDAY

I woke up early the next morning simultaneously excited and irritated. Excited because I was going to see Digs for dinner, and irritated because I had again forgotten to close the blinds and was awakened by a facefull of menacing sunshine.

After a long shower, a quick shave, and a rather average period of getting dressed, I headed out to get some breakfast. The weather was the same as the day before – beautiful – and I thought about heading to the Montgomery Street Café in Fort Worth. I settled for Whataburger (which on the fast food ranking scale is not settling at all).

Once I got there, I placed my order, got my drink, and sat down with a copy of the *Fort Worth Star-Telegram* (alternately known as the *Startlegram* or the *Star-Pentagram*). An older gentleman in a crisp Whataburger uniform brought me my order and asked if I would like any picante sauce for my taquitos. I said I would. He handed two containers to me, wished me a good morning, and headed back to the counter.

Reading the morning paper was still a ritual I enjoyed, even though I got the bulk of my news from the internet. The physical sensation of holding the paper, folding back the pages, and focusing on a story somehow pulled me out of whatever I was thinking about previously and allowed me to concentrate on the article's subject. I had always believed that letting go of the problem you were obsessed with was one of the keys to solving it, though I'm not sure I could ever prove that.

A good newspaper helped me with the process. This morning, though, there wasn't really anything to hold my attention. There were the prerequisite columns about the owner of the Dallas Cowboys being a complete, egomaniacal idiot, accompanied by a host of features about why this season might actually be their season. That was a pattern: the more vitriolic the column, the exponentially more positive features about the team, as if to make up for it. The Texas Rangers had became respectable, consistent contenders and post season regulars, but it could be Game 7 of the World Series and the Cowboys would be page one of the sports section, above the fold. Whatever.

There was nothing there to keep my attention off the case. After finishing the paper and my breakfast, I headed to the Hurst Police Department in the City of Hurst's government complex right off Airport Freeway.

I pulled into one of the parking spaces for visitors. Once inside, I let the female officer at the front desk know I was there to see Detective Baker. She asked me to wait just a few minutes. I took a seat in the waiting area. There were a number of magazines there: an old copy of *The FBI Law Enforcement Bulletin* (it was now an online publication), *Police Magazine*, *American Police Beat*, *Field & Stream*, *Bowhunter*, and *Cat Fancy*. I decided to inspect my shoes instead.

Ginger Baker turned out to be an attractive red head, about 5'7" with a lean, almost athletic build, green eyes and an "I can kick your ass, so don't even try it" kind of vibe. She opened the door behind the officer I had spoken to, leaned halfway out, and looked straight at me.

"Donovan Bay?" she asked, clearly thrilled to have her morning coffee interrupted by the likes of me.

I stood up, walked up to her and stuck out my hand. "Detective," I said. She had a firm handshake, always a plus.

"C'mon back," she said. She motioned me to follow her and I did.

"Nick Molsby told me you've been working the Hollander case. The victim's mother just hired me and it seemed like a good idea to touch base with you," I said. We ended up at her desk. Nicer than the old days, but hardly the lap of luxury. There were boxes of what looked to be current case files stacked slightly higher than her desktop piled next to her desk.

"Molsby told me you'd want to talk," she said as she sat down. She motioned to the empty chair next to the desk and I took a seat. "So I asked around and almost all of the guys here seem to think you're okay or better."

"Except for Tom Frederick," I said.

"Except for Tom Frederick," she said. "How is old Hollywood?"

"You the one that gave him that nickname?"

"I sort of think the universe did that."

"But you're the one that did it?"

I nodded.

"He's such a jerk," she said. A genuine smile. Nice. She

reached over and tapped my shoulder with her fist.

"We all have our bad days," I said.

"Coffee?" she motioned with her head as she picked up her own cup, still steaming. There was a fresh pot on top of a row of filing cabinets. I thanked her, but passed.

"So, what can I tell you about the Hollander case?" she asked.

"Anything come to mind? Did you ever have anyone you liked for it?"

"There were a few minor things, but nothing real. A couple of jerks that worked for him…"

"Like Larry Green?" I asked.

She smiled at me again and something said that I'd just been officially accepted.

"Very good," she said.

My rule was to let the person I was talking to tell me what they were going to say without a lot of interjection. One caveat to that was that it was fine to break the rule if the result was going to be more information. Dealing with police and other government officials, it was almost always better to be perceived as an insider, even an adversarial one, than as an outsider, even a friendly one.

Since I already had a copy of the files for this case – something I couldn't tell her – I was after the stuff that wasn't in the files, the opinions and hunches and feelings of those who investigated it when it was fresh. And since I'm pretty good at talking to people, that's what I got from Ginger Baker. Unfortunately it was pretty much the definition of "not much to go on."

She had been the first detective to respond to the scene, getting the call on the way to the office after a dental appointment. And she did have nice teeth, I thought.

From the beginning this one had been tough, she said, starting with the brutal nature of the attack. She had worked homicide in Dallas and seen some rough crime scenes, but the savageness of this one blew them away, even ones linked to the Mexican drug cartels. And as unforgettable as the crime scene was, the rest of the case was a series of dead ends.

No known enemies or outstanding quarrels. His parents and business associates had not been able to think of anyone who could have even remotely wanted or had cause to do such a thing. She brushed a few strands of hair from her eyes and looked at me.

"The only thing I kept coming back to – and that was purely because I couldn't come up with anything else – was that this was a guy without many personal friends. Lots of business friends. Tons. But it was like he worked *all* the time and didn't have anything left over for a social life," she said.

"You ever get any read that he mixed business with pleasure?"

"Yeah. One blip on the radar and that was it," she said. She opened the lid of the top box and pulled out a file. She started leafing through the pages, then stopped. She scanned down the page.

"There was this lady at his store in Arlington, Vivian Jenkins. She said that they dated a few times and that he even met her kid. She couldn't quite figure out why it didn't go anywhere."

I asked her if Jenkins had perceived any negative fallout from the relationship or non-relationship.

"Nope. No nothing. And I'm telling you, that was about the juiciest lead this case had to offer," she said.

I thanked her for her time and asked if I could touch base with her as I progressed with the case. She gave me one of her cards and she said not to hesitate to call. You know, the thing everyone always says but doesn't actually mean.

I told her I'd be in touch. I turned to leave and she put her hand on my forearm.

"This was a dead end from the beginning, the whole case. It took me a couple months to admit that. I was surprised by how much I liked his mom, though, so I kept at it. I'd be happy if you found something I missed," she said, "but I doubt you will."

CHAPTER 13

The thought of seeing Digs sent my pulse racing and lifted my spirits, though after a day of looking at the files and crime scene photos from this case, my spirits didn't have anyplace to go but up. None of that mattered. The circumstances didn't matter, though. She had always had that effect on me. I laughed at myself because I felt like a teenager, and I disliked teenagers even when I was one.

The ease of our conversation the previous night made me question the last few years. Maybe I should have ended the silence. Maybe the timing was simply perfect now. Maybe I was a complete moron who just needed to slow down. I liked her a whole lot more than she liked me. It had always been that way. I would never put up with that from anyone else. Why did I with her?

In all the time that had passed since I last saw her, I never stopped thinking of Digs O'Conner as one of my best friends. If she had called me, I would have dropped just about anything or anyone and come running.

But she hadn't called either.

I was still thinking about it when I rang her doorbell.

The angst all faded away when I saw her smile. Years melted away and I found myself unable to not smile back. I tried to say "How are you, Digs?" but she was on me with one of the fierce hugs she was known for in high school.

"So where are you taking me for dinner?" she whispered in my ear as if she had been saying something far more suggestive. It would have made a lesser man buckle. I chuckled and she threw her head back and laughed loudly.

"I am so glad to see you!" she said.

Maybe time healed all wounds or maybe I was an idiot who should have called her much sooner without waiting for something trivial like the city's most vicious unsolved murder case ever to prompt me. I don't know.

I asked her if she'd ever been to Longoria's in Colleyville.

She said she'd never been there, which was her way of telling me that she had but wouldn't mind going again. She closed her door behind her and we walked to my car. Even without looking directly at her, I could feel her smiling. I opened the passenger door for her, she got in, and I closed it. As I crossed behind the car and got in the driver's side, I couldn't stop smiling.

I started up the car, dropped it in gear, and pulled away from the curb.

"So, you finally got one? This is a 1964 ½ Mustang, right? I nodded like I was cool.

"You've been talking about this car as long as I've known you," she said. "How'd you finally get it?"

"Two years ago I took a case for a big auto auction. I turned the thing pretty quickly for them. That led to another job and that, in turn, put me in good with the owner, who put me onto this," I said, motioning with my hands as I drove.

"I'm no more mechanically inclined than I was before, but I did the interior restoration myself and I've got an awesome mechanic in Euless for the rest," I said.

"It's great, Donovan. It totally suits you," she said as we turned onto Grapevine Highway. I stepped firmly on the gas and the car responded with power.

"This car would have been wasted on you when you were talking about it back in high school," she said.

"More like I wouldn't have known what to do with the girls I would have gotten back then," I said.

"But you would have probably figured it out."

"See, that's what makes me such a world class private investigator," I said.

"Oh, is that it?" she asked.

I nodded yes.

We pulled into the restaurant's parking lot, parked, and went inside. We were seated and had our menus in hand with drinks on the way almost immediately. Digs ordered the carne asada with an enchilada on the side, and a Margarita. I made it two.

We spent the next hour talking about what old friends were doing now, who we still ran into, and how differently life had turned than what we expected. We talked about my family and hers.

"My niece, Rhonda – David's daughter, I don't think you ever met her – moved to Bedford about three years ago with her mom and stepdad. She's going to Bell and she's over at my place all the time now. Not so much because I'm spoiling her, but because I'm just not her parents," she said.

David was Digs and her twin sister Juliet's older brother. He was in his late 20s and serving in the U.S. Army's special forces when I first met the girls. He was killed about 10 years back on a mission that had yet to be declassified, leaving behind a wife and a young daughter, Rhonda.

Digs pulled out her phone and flipped through photos of her and her niece. There was definitely a family resemblance, and it was clear that they were quite close.

Rhonda being in high school was yet another reminder that we all age. Digs said she had always missed being a regular part of her niece's life, and she was really enjoying them living so close.

"She's not my kid, but she's my kid," she said as she looked at one of the photos.

The meal was superb and it was still early when we finished. We decided to head back to her place. I hadn't forgotten that I still had some work-related questions for her.

Digs made a cup of coffee for herself and handed me a cold can of Dr. Pepper.

"You have no idea how appalling it is to me to offer a guest a drink in a can. It reminds me of waiting tables, and I *hated* waiting tables," she said.

"I'm too low brow for you, Digs."

"Probably," she said as she settled into a chair opposite mine. "So, what's this big high school question you need to ask me?"

"You have your yearbooks?"

"Sure, mine and Juliet's, at least until she retires from the Army or gets based near here."

"How's she doing?"

"She sounds good whenever we talk, but you know her. You can't really tell how she is or what she's thinking unless you're looking at her," she said.

"I always sort of thought as you guys got older that you'd be more twin-like, if that's the right adjective. I mean, seriously, aside from looking alike…"

"I know. I love her and I look just like her, but we are pretty different, aren't we?" she asked.

"Not quite day and night, but not far off," I said.

She got up and walked to the bookshelf. Pictures of Rhonda at various ages stood in the open spots on the shelves. She asked me which yearbook I wanted.

"Let me see the year I graduated."

She went right to it, pulled it off the shelf, turned around and handed it to me. I flipped through the pages until I found the French club. I held the book up so she could see it:

"You remember this photo?"

"Sure."

"A copy of this book was open to this very page at the scene of Roger Hollander's murder," I said.

She blinked in confusion, disbelief. "What?"

"Yeah, weird, I know."

"How do you even know that?"

"I was looking at an enlargement of one of the crime scene photos. I spotted it. I have no idea what the chances of it happening to be something I worked on, but even upside down

I recognized it. The question I have is *why*?"

"That is so… creepy, Donovan."

"That I recognized it?"

"I hadn't thought about Roger in years before I heard about his murder. And now you're telling me he was looking at this photo that I was in?" She sat back down across from me again.

"Well, either he was or his killer was." I hadn't thought about it before I said it. That made me pause.

"What? Do you think it has something to do with the photo? Am I in some kind of danger?"

I reached out and touched her arm.

"No, I don't think so. Don't forget, this happened more than year ago. If you were in danger, I think you'd have known it by now. What I really want to figure out is why a guy who graduated four years ahead of me had this yearbook."

She looked at me like I was confusing her. "What?" I asked.

"He got the yearbook after I showed him how many pictures there were of me in it," she said. "He and I were dating at the time. Don't you remember?"

CHAPTER 14

"Son of a bitch," I said. "I completely forgot all that."

I had no doubt the World Class Private Investigator Certification Bureau would be calling to take back their genuine, suitable-for-framing certificate. You know, if there was such a thing.

Damn it. Now I remembered. I had only ever seen the guy at a distance a couple of times and met him once. It was in the kitchen at Digs' parents' house. My only defense was that it was two decades ago and I disliked most of the guys she dated. The guy was more or less a ghost to me.

Of course, that was at the time in high school I was dating Laura Field, so I could forgive myself a little if Digs fell ever so slightly off my radar. I mean, seriously, *I* fell off my radar for a while during that time.

I shook the thought and got back to the matter at hand.

"When did you start seeing him?"

"I think it was probably right before school started your senior year. I met him in August of that year, when he came in the restaurant where Jules and I were working," she said. She had known him in passing through some of her friends. He had dated Karen Crosby – who I actually did remember – but they had broken up at the beginning of that summer. Neither of them had been dating anyone at the time and things picked up pretty quickly.

"Didn't that make him like, what 22, and you 16?"

"And I'm sure you don't remember saying that at the time either?" she smiled.

"No, I don't remember it," I said, "but it sure sounds like me."

We sat quietly for a moment, one that no doubt seemed longer to her as I tried to jog the pieces of my memory back into place.

"Like you didn't date anyone younger?" she raised an eyebrow.

"What?" I was lost again.

"Terry Freeman?"

"Geez, Digs, she was 14 and I was 17. That's not that big a difference," I said.

"And she was a mature 14."

"If by 'mature' you meant 'active and aggressive,' okay. If by 'mature' you actually meant 'mature,' I have to say it was more like I was an immature 17," I said, "but I get your point."

"So, it's not a crime, but it's not exactly like you were Peter Pureheart at that time," she said. "I could use another drink. How about you?"

"Okay," I said.

"I have a couple bottles of a nice red wine I just discovered, or if you don't want to mix things up I could whip up a couple of margaritas pretty quickly," she said.

We settled on margaritas and she went into her kitchen to make them. I got up, went to her sofa, and stretched out. I kicked off my shoes and each one fell to the floor with a thunk. I looked at the texture of the ceiling and the slowly spinning blades of her ceiling fan.

It was really beginning to piss me off. I remembered the day I met this girl. I remembered picking her up every day from school once I got my license and giving her a ride home and often to work after that. I remembered cringe-worthy conversations in which I said stupid, cringe-worthy, teenager-y things. If you had asked me 20 minutes earlier, I would have said I remembered virtually everything about her from that time.

Nick Molbsy would have me pegged as an unreliable witness. And he'd be right. I didn't like it, but that's how it was. The sooner I let go of it, the better it would be for the case.

"You know I'm just making a point bringing up Terry Freeman, right?" she asked as she came back into the room carrying our drinks. "Oh, and just make yourself at home, right?"

I sat up and took my drink from her.

"Donovan, I'm just kidding. Stretch out. I was actually just going to say how cool it was to hang out with you. It's like I saw you five days ago, not five years," she clinked the edge of her glass against mine. "And that's special."

"Here, here!" I said and clinked her glass back.

She sat down on the sofa beside me.

"So, tell me about the stuff I don't remember. I've made

my peace with this gaping hole in my otherwise superior memory..." I lied.

"What don't you remember about Terry Freeman?"

"Funny. About you and Roger Hollander. How long did you guys see each other?"

"About a year. It was pretty nice at first. I liked the attention from an older guy. I was really tired of how immature most of the guys I knew were. Jules was fine whether she had a boyfriend or not. We were definitely not twins in that regard. Anyhow, I was majorly in love and writing his name in my notebook and all that, but it reached a plateau and..."

"He wasn't going to be 'the one' after all?"

"Yeah, you could definitely say that."

"How did it end?"

"It sort of just fizzled." She took a long sip of her margarita. "Hey, not bad! You should try it."

I took a long sip, too. She was right. "Nice," I said. "How'd it end?"

"I got busier with school and activities. He wanted more of my time than I had to give. That sort of thing," she said.

She leaned over and put her head on my shoulder and took my hand in hers.

"I'm really glad to see you tonight, Donovan. But could we not talk about Roger anymore this evening? I'm a little creeped out the book being opened to the photo."

I told her that I was sure I'd have some more questions, but that they could definitely wait.

We sat there like that in silence for several minutes, then she turned and looked at me with a quizzical expression.

"What did you ever see in Terry Freeman?"

"Boobs," I said with a shrug.

"Well, that's hard to argue with," she laughed and took another long sip. I put my arm around her and we sat there some more.

CHAPTER 15

As I was on my way out of Digs' place, my phone rang. It was Laura Field. She told me that she had multiple articles on the murder for me to look at, but they didn't really have anything new for me. I grumbled.

"Such is the state of reporting today," she said.

I asked her to keep looking and told her I might have more information for her to comb through the following day. I got in my car and closed the door with a solid thump.

"Where are you?" she asked.

"Just leaving Digs' place."

"Really?"

"Look at me. The social butterfly, 20 years removed," I said as I put the key in the ignition and started the car.

"I haven't seen her in ages. How is she?"

"It was good to see her."

"Got time to stop by?"

"Laura, I'm really beat," I said.

"Just for a few minutes."

"Okay, I said. Be there in 10." I hung up. In my mind, I headed for home and a good night's sleep. In reality, I headed for Laura's house and whatever she was going to do to my brain that would make me unable to sleep because I couldn't stop thinking about it. Not that she had done that before or anything.

The 10-minute drive took me 17 minutes, because I hit a drive-through for a Dr. Pepper. I needed some caffeine. I pulled into the driveway at Laura's house, shut off the car, walked up to the front door and rang the bell.

The speaker by the doorbell crackled. "Donovan?"

"Probably," I said back.

"Then I'll probably be right there."

A minute later I heard the deadbolt slide and the doorknob turn.

"C'mon in," she said.

She turned around and left me to close the door, which I did. If there was such a thing as retro punk pajamas, she was wearing them, along with her glasses with oversized frames instead of her usual contacts.

"How's Digs?"

"She seemed good. Very Digs-like. Turns out she dated Roger Hollander in high school," I said as we entered her home office.

"Well, that's not weird or anything," she said, which was Laura-speak for "That's pretty weird." She picked a large book up off the chair next to hers so I could sit down. She looked at me skeptically.

"She's two years younger than me and he was four years older than me," she said quietly. Then: "Ewww."

"When I brought that up, she threw Terry Freeman at me."

"Not literally?"

"Nope."

"Because *that* would have been weird."

I conceded the point.

"I might have done the same thing if I was trying to distract you from the idea that I had dated a pedophile when I was in high school," she said.

"What?"

"I'm exaggerating for effect," she admitted.

I sat down and she handed me a file three times the size of the one I had given her. "He was a senior at University of North Texas dating a sophomore at L.D. Bell High School. Ten years later, that age difference wouldn't mean much. But at that age, Donovan, that's actually squarely on the creepy side."

"How creepy?"

"Pretty creepy," she said. "Anyhow, let's just run through this stuff really quickly. As I said on the phone, it's mostly what you've read before. There are some more details, but probably nothing you haven't worked out already…"

She stopped suddenly.

"Do you think I ought to talk to my cousin?"

Non-Sequitur Theater, as I called it, was Laura's specialty.

"What?" I asked.

"I really think she might have dated this guy when they were in high school together."

"Who? Your cousin? Really?"

She started nodding. "Yeah, I think she did."

"I guess it couldn't hurt," I said. "Just let me know what

she says."

Laura shrugged her agreement and went back to pointing out a few details in the articles. She flipped through a few more pages in the folder. She told me to read them just in case I saw something she didn't. Then she came to the last few pages. She pulled them out of the folder and spread them on her desk.

They were Roger Hollander's financials. They might be in the police reports, but if they were, I hadn't seen them yet.

"How did you get these, Laura?"

"Remember how I tracked down the original deed documents for that high-end housing development off of Cheek Sparger Road by finding that guy's great grandson?"

"Yeah...?"

"Steve Harris at the bank remembered, too," she said.

"Well, I hope you didn't waste a favor on a dead-end case."

"We'll see. I still have a lot to do. In the meantime, I thought you'd like to take a look at the basics."

Roger Hollander, to put it mildly, was really well off. The number of zeroes in his bank account was impressive. Unlike mine, his had the benefit of other numbers to the left of the zeroes. I let out a small whistle.

"I know his parents have money and everything, but doesn't that seem like a lot from just a cell phone business, even a successful one?"

"I don't know. Does it?"

"Yeah, it sort of does. Not saying there's anything wrong with it. It just caught my attention. That's all," she said.

"Look into it. See what you can find. I have another guy who can help us run some of it if your Steve Harris can't help," said.

I rubbed my eyes and looked at my watch. No wonder I was so tired.

"I've got to get to bed," I said.

"Thought you'd never ask," she said. She looked up from her notes with a smile. I chuckled, kissed her on the top of her head, thanked her for the work and told her I'd call her tomorrow.

She saw me to the door and watched me walk out to my car. I waved a tired goodnight to her. She smiled, waved and winked at me, then closed the door as I started the car. I saw the porch light go out.

I dropped the car into gear and finally headed for home. On the way, I pretended not to be thinking of her. Once I got to my place, despite Digs, Laura, the caffeine, and the case, I managed to sleep the sleep of the dead.

CHAPTER 16

THURSDAY

Even the all-out assault of sunlight through the once again unclosed blinds in my bedroom didn't wake me up until about 20 minutes after I was normally at the office. I picked up the phone and called the office hoping Michelle would answer. She did.

"Glad you're there. I just woke up."

"What's her name?" she asked.

"Her name is stayed up working late last night."

"What's her last name?"

"Did you read over the case files?"

"Sure did. Ready to chat about them whenever you decide to roll your rear end into the office, Donovan," she said.

"I have to get ready and I want to call Mrs. Hollander, so I'd guess I'd be there in an hour or less. See you then."

I hung up and then sat up on the bed, putting my feet on the floor. It wasn't quite a hangover, I really was only accustomed to drinking beer, so I had a slight headache. A hot shower and lots of water would solve that.

* * *

I turned on the shower then drank a cold bottle of water while I was waiting for the water to heat up. Why that took so long in a state as hot as Texas, science might never know. Soon enough I climbed in and let water cascade over my head, down my back and all over. I stood under the hot spray and let it hit my neck. I felt the dull ache start to leave me. I rolled my head slowly from side to side, soaking in the heat, stretching very passively.

After about 10 minutes of that, I finished up quickly, then lowered the temperature of the water a bit. I began to wake up in earnest. I turned off the shower, climbed out, grabbed a towel, dried off, wrapped the towel around me and started to shave. That took about a minute. I drank some more water, got dressed, and got ready to go.

When I was ready, I sat down at my desk and called Mrs. Hollander. She sounded pleased to hear from me. I told her that I talked to managers in several of their locations now, but I wondered if Roger had an assistant or business manager, someone who knew the ins and outs of the whole operation at the time.

She told me that would be Donna Mahaffey, who was still with the company and was working with Hollander's father in a similar capacity. She gave me a cell phone number for her and an office number. She also said I could just stop by the office and talk with Mahaffey if I wanted to do so.

* * *

As I was leaving my place and walking to my car, my phone rang. It was Laura.

"Talked to my cousin. I was right. She remembered all the

details right away. She was a year younger than him. Said the guy seemed nice enough, but he was all handsy very quickly. When she tried to slow it down, he more or less dumped her," she said.

"Sounds like a lot of high school age jerks."

"He dumped her in favor of a girl in junior high. But it's... This just feels like we might talking about a pattern here," she said.

"Anything else?"

"Yeah, all of that and she still thought he was very good looking."

"Thanks, Laura."

I climbed into the car, closed the door and started it up. The engine roared to life and then idled with a purr. I dropped it into gear and headed for the office, with an intermediate stop for breakfast built into the plan.

CHAPTER 17

I had hit the drive-through at Whataburger for a couple taquitos. I ate them on the way to the office, despite my paranoia about spilling anything in my car. It turned out to be a good thing because Michelle was talking to another new client when I walked through the door.

She quickly introduced me to Jeff Veytia, owner of a comic book shop called ESC Key Comics in Euless. Mr. Veytia had recently had several high dollar back issues go missing. The two most likely suspects were a pair of longtime employees.

Veytia was tall and lean, though not skinny. At a quick guess, I said about 6'3" and 200 pounds, give or take. He had jet black hair, a little bit of scar on his right cheek, and an athletic build. He had that look that people get when they've spent too much time proving their reality was real to the disbelieving rest of society.

I asked if he had gone to the police and he said he had. Both employees had been looked at by the Euless Police Department and had even volunteered to take polygraphs. They had been cleared, but he still thought otherwise. The missing issues had not turned up in any local sales or on the internet. The investigation was ongoing, but he didn't feel like the Euless officers really understood the nature of the crime.

"High end comics are big business these days," I said. "What's missing?"

"A copy of *Amazing Fantasy* #15 graded 9.2 and a copy *Tales of Suspense* #39, also graded 9.4," he said.

There was an air of "And I'm sure you don't know what that means…" in the way he said it.

"And I'm willing to bet Euless guys didn't believe you when you told them the combined values were in the neighborhood of $500,000, right?"

Mr. Veytia blinked at me a few times.

"Yeah…What?" he almost literally shook his head in a double take. "No, they totally didn't get it. My insurance guy even came over and showed them *The Overstreet Comic Book Price Guide*. Finally one of their sergeants turned out to be one of my customers and he backed me up."

"But even after they realized that this is a pretty high dollar crime, no results?"

"Nothing," he said.

He proceeded to tell us about the two employees, Max Norman and Bebe Ally. They were a college-age couple. They had met at his store and fallen in love while working together. Mr. Veytia said he'd be happy to be proven wrong.

But he didn't think he was wrong. I had nothing against the cops in Euless (well, let's call it almost nothing), but I didn't have nearly the rapport with them that I did with the guys in Hurst. I also had told Mrs. Hollander that we didn't have anything on our plate.

"We have an operative who knows your world pretty well, Mr. Veytia," I said. I turned and looked toward Michelle. "Have you talked rates yet?"

"We sure have," she said. "And he would like us to start right away."

* * *

After Mr. Veytia left, I asked Michelle to put in a call to Tyler Newsup, who worked for us on a case by case basis. Tyler was jack of many – if not all – trades and a pop culture junkie of the highest order. With his help, I was confident we could take this case on top the one we already had. When it rains, it pours, of course, but you always know another drought is coming, so you take the work while you can get it.

"Have him call me on my cell," I told her. "I'm going over to Roger Hollander's office to talk with some of the folks there."

"You still have to fill me in on your date the other night," she said as I was headed out the door.

"It wasn't a date," I called back over my shoulder.

"Yeah, right," I heard her say.

* * *

Hollander's headquarters, which was also his company's warehouse, was a clean, but almost soulless box building. Aside from being in good repair, its true redeeming feature was that it was part of a small business development that had replaced a shopping center that had been mostly dead for 20 years.

There were plenty of open parking spaces, so I took one

near the door that was under the company's sign. As soon as I was inside, I was greeted by a lady behind the front desk. Her name tag said "Inez."

"Hello, sir, how can I help you?" she said. Even after spending three quarters of my life in Texas, it still weirded me out when people older than me called me "sir," but it was just a form of respect. I love Texas even more than I love Taco Bueno.

"Yes, ma'm. I'm looking for Donna Mahaffey, if she's in. Mrs. Hollander suggested I speak to her." I handed Inez one of my cards.

She eyed it and seemed to take it pretty seriously.

"Oh, my," she said. "She was on a call a few minutes ago. Let me run up and see if she's still on it or not. Can I get you some coffee or water while you wait?"

"Water sounds good."

There was a row of seats arranged against the wall facing the counter at which Inez sat. I grabbed a seat while she brought me a cold bottle of water.

"I'll be right back," she said. She clanged up the metal stairs to the building's second floor. Then I could hear her shoes echo across the floor and eventually diminish. I looked around as I sat there. The office area on the first floor had windows that faced onto the warehouse floor. Out there, there were racks extending almost the full two stories of the building's height. I saw a forklift buzz by the office windows and a moment later go back the other way with a shrink-wrapped pallet on its lift.

Inez came clanging quickly back down the stairs. She told me that Donna Mahaffey was just about done with her phone call and that if I wouldn't mind waiting a few minutes, she'd be glad to talk with me. I thanked her.

"Is this about the Hollanders' son?" she asked quietly.

I nodded.

"I never knew him. I started about two weeks after he died. I like his father, though, and I've met Mrs. Hollander a few times, too. She seems very nice," she said.

"People around here say very much about Roger?"

"Not really," she said. "I think everyone's just sort of sensitive about not wanting to hurt anyone's feelings."

I nodded again. From her reaction, I'm sure it came across as approval. I was just making mental notes. The phone on Inez's desk buzzed and she jumped a little. She picked it up, said "Hello," and then just listened for a moment and hung up.

"Donna will see you now, Mr. Bay. Top of the stairs, turn left, and she's the third door on the left," she said.

I thanked her and headed upstairs.

CHAPTER 18

Donna Mahaffey was beautiful. That was my first observation when I entered her office, and that in turn made me wonder if Hollander had made any advances toward her, welcomed or not. Given his mixed track record to this point, I would have guessed yes. And if I had been in his place, I would have been at least interested because I was at least interested right now.

"Come in, Mr. Bay," she said from behind her desk. As I walked toward her desk, she got up from behind it and came walking toward me. She had long, dark hair, an attractive build, a beautiful smile, and killer eyes. And a good handshake. Think Catherine Zeta Jones, circa *Zorro*.

She wore a gray pantsuit, black 3" heels, and a very light pink blouse. The jacket that matched the slacks hung on a rack in one of the corners. She had several different file folders open and spread out across her desk.

"Thanks for seeing me. Mrs. Hollander said you might be able to give me a look back at how things worked around here when her son was running the business," I said. She offered me the seat opposite hers and I took it.

"I'll be glad to tell you whatever I can, Mr. Bay."

"How were the overall operations handled?"

"This part hasn't changed much, particularly since Mr. Hollander's father doesn't care for day-to-day functions. Roger handled strategic planning. He focused on expanding the business. He kept his hand in the daily activities of the stores by spot inspections. The nuts and bolts part of the business, the standard ordering of product and the like, he left to me. That's what I'm doing still," she said.

"Who took care of the finances?"

"On the daily activities, that would be a few people who reported to me, but in terms of signing leases for space or really significant purchases, Roger would have handled that. In that area, I've taken over a little more since he left, though his father doesn't mind evaluating potential retail spaces," she said.

I asked a lot of questions and very quickly had developed the feeling that she was a focused person who knew her job very well. She seemed assured without being arrogant, a fine line to walk in this hyper-sensitive world, and a finer line to walk for a woman.

As she answered each of the questions, her confidence never ebbed or faded. She clearly knew the operation backward and forward, which is what you expect of someone in her position and yet so rarely find. Forgetting for a moment how she looked, I would have hired her for the job if I was the one interviewing. I just like when people seem to know their jobs and are good at them. It's appealing. It makes me want to do business with them.

"I don't want to make it sound like Roger wasn't involved in operations. He didn't mind jumping in and making a delivery to a store, doing customer service follow-ups, or anything. He would do whatever was needed, but he didn't want to be tied to those kinds of activities on a regular basis," she said.

I changed to subject to his relationships with his employees.

"Well, of course the ones he knew best were the managers and assistant managers, who tended to come over here to our headquarters a little more, but he also got to know some of the people in our stores, too," she said.

"Some a bit more than others?"

"Well, perhaps some…" she stopped. "Wait. What?"

"Ms. Mahaffey, I've noticed that a number of female employees have seemed to imply that Roger made what might be considered inappropriate advances toward them and that some of those who responded favorably to this were given preferential treatment over those who didn't," I said.

She paused for a moment, caught off guard. If she hadn't been so impressive on everything else, I would have missed it. It was that fleeting.

"I can't think of anyone who has had that experience," she said.

"How about Lisa Jefferson?" I asked.

A second pause, just a couple of blinks long. Then she smiled.

"Perhaps, I should restate my previous answer, Mr. Bay," she said. "While I cannot speak about the specific details of the situation, I can confirm that Mr. Hollander was indeed briefly involved with Ms. Jefferson. The situation was not as you describe, but we did reach a mutually agreeable settlement with her regarding her departure from the firm."

"As comfortably as you said that, I bet you're what passes for the in-house legal counsel," I said.

She just smiled.

"And I bet you don't want to say anymore about it."

"Not a matter of want to or don't want to," she said. "Under the terms of the settlement, neither side can discuss the matter further."

"Okay, so for the moment we'll set aside Ms. Jefferson. I've spoken with a number of your employees at across several of your stores, and I've also talked with women who knew Roger outside of work. There's something of a pattern developing," I said.

"Does Mrs. Hollander know that this is your line of questioning? How could indulging in this sort of muck-raking in anyway help find out who killed him?" Her smile and professional demeanor were starting to slip just a bit, but I thought it was impressive that they were there at all.

"I give Mrs. Hollander regular reports on the investigation, Ms. Mahaffey, and she remains very interested in finding her son's killer. The police didn't come up with many likely suspects, so I'm looking at everyone's possible motives. I don't do it to be provocative," I lied. "I ask these questions because *someone* killed Roger Hollander and that didn't happen without a motive."

She nodded slowly, calmly.

"Alright," she said. "I see your point. What else can I tell you?"

"Did Roger ever put the moves on you?"

"No."

"Did you ever see him put the moves on anyone else?"

"No."

"Could you imagine the circumstance in which he would do such a thing?"

"No."

"Okay. Thank-you," I said and stood up. "If you think of anything that might help, particularly anyone who might have had a reason to be angry with Roger, let me know."

I handed her one of my cards and she took it. The professional composure was back. She smiled again, but she put my card on her desk without looking at it. I thanked her again for her time and left, clanking down the stairs as I went. I waved and said goodbye to Inez at the front desk.

Outside, I walked to my car, got in, and checked my phone. Tyler Newsup had called while I was inside. I jotted his name down on a notepad and called Michelle.

"Just talked with Donna Mahaffey at Hollander's office. I think we're onto something with Roger's relationships with female employees," I said.

"Okay. Maybe you ought to come in and talk about it," she said.

"Will do. I'm going to call Tyler back and see when I can meet with him," I said. "Then we'll talk about Roger's supposedly non-existent dating life."

CHAPTER 19

I met Tyler Newsup at the Denny's in Euless at the intersection of Highway 183 and Highway 157. It was enough before lunch and enough past breakfast that it was easy to get a table. I asked for an unsweetened ice tea and Tyler ordered the same as the hostess handed us each a menu.

"You ever have lunch with Molsby?" Tyler asked as if we'd already exchanged greetings.

"Sure. Recently, in fact," I said.

"What's his deal about calling waiters 'dude waitresses?'" He made the air quotes motion with two fingers on each hand.

"Never noticed it," I said while looking more intently at the menu.

"Thought as much," he said, looking at his. The waitress, a smiling young lady named Monikay according to her name tag, came over and took our order. Having eaten breakfast already, I requested a bowl of fruit. Tyler ordered scrambled eggs with pepperoni, hash browns, a side of bacon, and wheat toast. After he said "wheat toast," he turned and looked at me and told me he had to watch what he ate. He did so because he was appallingly in shape despite eating in one day as much bad food as I ate in a week or perhaps two. He knew I'd rather have what he was having. At least I liked fruit.

Tyler was thin, but not skinny or wiry. He had a toughness about him that was hard to miss, but he could subvert it and play the nebbish when he was undercover. He was one of those people who could perfectly blend into just about any crowd. People who described him would tend to transpose onto him the features or styles they wanted to see. He was a walking dichotomy, and he was perfect for the case at hand.

"So, what's the case, Cochise?" he said. "Michelle didn't give me much to go on." He poured two packets of sugar into his ice tea.

"Why do you get unsweetened ice tea and then sweeten it?"

"Because they do it wrong. What's the case?"

"ESC Key Comics up on Euless Main. Owner's name is Veytia," I said.

"I know him. It's not my regular store. It's my emergency back-up store. I'm in there enough that he knows me to see me, but I don't have a pull list there, so I bet he doesn't remember my name," he said.

"Emergency back-up store?"

"Sure. As a serious collector – "

"And you are."

" – and I am – you have a regular store where you usually get your stuff. You have what's called a pull list or standing order. Now if their distributor shorts them on something you've ordered, you can wait until it catches up with you at your regular store," he finished stirring his tea and took a long sip. "But if it's an item that's highly in demand and you think they might not get a second shipment, then you have a back-up store."

"Okay," I shrugged.

"See, the thing is, if an item is in high demand in one store, it very well could be in the other store as well, so you have to be familiar to the back-up store as well or they'll think you only come there for the rare, hot stuff, and they'll save it for one of their regulars," he said.

"Buying comic books sounds a lot more complicated than I expected."

"Of course that's only talking about new stuff. I take it this concerns older back issues or it wouldn't be worth your time or mine."

Monikay brought our orders. She set Tyler's plate down in front of him and asked if he wanted any ketchup, hot sauce or anything. He asked for Tabasco and she pulled a small bottle from her apron and set it next to his plate. She set my bowl of fruit down and gave me a look that said, "That's just sort of sad…" as she asked if she could get us anything else.

"You're right," I said to Tyler as Monikay walked away. "*Amazing Fantasy* #15 and *Tales of Suspense* #39, both high grade. Michelle will send you the notes from our conversation with Jeff Veytia. He thinks it's an inside job. Euless cops don't, and they don't seem to be taking it very seriously."

His phone pinged.

"Is she listening in?" he asked.

"What?"

"That was Michelle just sending me the notes."

I smiled.

"So, how do you want this to go?"

"Standard rates. Michelle may be available a bit if you need back-up on anything. For the most part, except to talk, I'm on another case full time," I said. "But I do want you to keep me in the loop."

"I know. I know. No 'Tandoori chicken' incident," he said, making air quotes again. I nodded my agreement.

Tyler had finished his entire breakfast as I was still working on my third piece of pineapple. He motioned for Monikay to bring him another ice tea and she waved back.

"I can start right after we're done here," he said.

CHAPTER 20

I called Michelle from the Denny's parking lot and confirmed that Tyler was on board. I gave her a few of the details about my meeting with Donna Mahaffey and told her that I thought I better check in with Mrs. Hollander before I headed back to the office.

"The more I think about it, I've been laying on the story of Roger's relationships a bit thick, particularly when half the time I've been bluffing. Sooner or later that's going to get back to her and it'd go better for us if it came from me," I said.

"Sounds about right," she said. "Are you heading here after that?"

I told her I would, then hung up. I saw Tyler start up his car, a dark colored recent model Jeep. He backed out of his space and then drove to the exit that would take him toward Main Street in Euless. I decided to head up the service road that way and head down Main Street myself. Then I'd take the back way to the Hollander residence in Bedford. The parking lot was a mess and I had to weave my way around a beat-up old El Camino that had at some point been a bronze-ish color, a bright yellow Volkswagen Beetle, and a silver Chevy pick-up truck with tinted windows.

"I'm too cool to be seen in a pick-up truck," I sang to myself as I threaded the space between the pick-up and the Beetle, neither of which were going to be able to move until the El Camino decided to get it in gear. I tried giving the driver a courtesy wave – you know, the lost art – but he or she just revved the engine at me. Whatever.

Once I escaped the parking lot, I made it up the service road, turned left onto the bridge over the highway and down Euless Main. I passed the fast food corridor and then saw Tyler's car at ESC Key Comics. I kept going until I got away from the construction zone and then started working my way toward Bedford.

* * *

Mrs. Hollander was just coming back from a walk when I pulled up in front of the house. Before her mind got racing, I told her I didn't have any news, that I just wanted to ask her a few more questions. She said that she needed to get a drink of water and invited me into the house. I sat down at the kitchen table and she got each of us a cold glass of filtered water. It tasted great. She sat down at the table with me.

"Mrs. Hollander, as I told you previously, I've been going over a lot of the ground the police went over before, but my approach is most likely going to be different than theirs," I said.

"Yes," she said and nodded.

"When we talked originally, you said that he wasn't in a relationship, but I should have asked the question more broadly. I seem to be getting some indications that Roger did have some relationships with women and that at least one of them ended a bit questionably," I said.

"That Lisa Jefferson woman," she almost spat. She sat silent for just a moment. "I wasn't trying to hide anything when we spoke, Mr. Bay."

"Farthest thing from my mind, Mrs. Hollander."

"Call me Jean, please."

"Okay, Jean. I just want to let you know, that I don't think you were hiding anything. I know you want to catch your son's killer no matter what, and that most likely neither Ms. Jefferson nor anyone else he may have seen at work or outside of work will turn out to have been involved. I just want you to be aware that I am going to pursue every angle I can think of, and this is part of that effort."

She looked like she wanted to say something. She took a drink of her water. I took a drink of mine.

"I appreciate you pushing beyond where the police have gone, Donovan. I know about my son's previous relationship with Miss Jefferson, but as far as I know that was resolved more or less amicably months and months before Roger's death. And while I'm sure he could have gone out with any number of women without me knowing about them, I did know my son and he wasn't seriously involved with anyone at the time of his death," she said.

"I just wanted you to hear this from me, rather than from someone whose toes I've stepped on in the process," I said.

She smiled.

"You're a good boy, Donovan. A good man. Keep going."

I told her I would. She had a charity luncheon to get ready for, so I finished my glass of water and showed myself out.

* * *

I walked down from the house to where my car was parked. As I was about to get in, I looked straight ahead to the end of the block. On the opposite side of the road, just across the intersection, sat a silver Chevy pick-up. It could have been the one from the Denny's parking lot, but it was a long block and I was too far away to get the license plate number.

The Dallas/Fort Worth Metroplex has about six and a half million people in it, but the Hurst-Euless-Bedford had less than 175,000 combined, each town having less than 60,000. That meant it wasn't entirely unreasonable to find yourself coming across the same vehicle a few times in the space of a day if you were out on the roads.

So maybe it was nothing. And maybe it wasn't.

I climbed into my car, popped the key the ignition and started it up. With my left hand on the steering wheel and my right hand on the gear shift, I started rolling toward the pick-up. With its windows tinted, I couldn't see the driver, but he or she could see me starting to pay attention. The truck turned left, accelerated suddenly, and was gone from my view.

I accelerated quickly down the street. I paused only long enough to look around the corner, and then I made the right turn to follow, again stomping on the gas. There was a short stretch of road before a variety of side streets knifed off in a variety of directions.

The silver pick-up was nowhere to be seen. I circled through the area in a changing pattern, but came up empty. Maybe it was nothing, I told myself. I didn't believe that for a minute.

CHAPTER 21

Sometimes you can't tell if someone's just a jerk or if they're being a jerk for a reason. There was no way to know for certain that the Silver pick-up truck with tinted windows had anything to do with anything or not. Coincidences do exist; they're just a lot more rare than people think.

Even after I said I was giving up, I made a few more passes on the streets surrounding the Hollander residence. It was an upscale, suburban development, a mix of nice older homes and pricey McMansions built too close to the ones next door for my taste. There was nothing going on, so I gave up for real and headed for the office. I called Michelle and let her know I was finally on my way. She said that Tyler had already made contact with Jeff Veytia at ESC Key Comics and that he'd be in touch later.

* * *

Fifteen minutes later I pulled in the parking lot at the office. Before I went upstairs to our office, I stopped in Carl's Deli and purchased a wonderfully cold can of Dr. Pepper and a bag of pretzels. Then I trotted up the stairs, opened the door to our office, and went in. Michelle was hanging up from a phone call.

"So, have you gone out with Digs again yet?" she asked.

"Since the last time we talked? That was like 17 minutes ago."

"Are you going to see her again?"

"Aren't you too busy destroying your own social life to start worrying about mine?" I put my drink and the bag of pretzels on my desk.

"Probably, but it's not like that would stop me. Do you guys have plans to go out again or not?"

"No." I sat down at my desk. I looked at Michelle for a moment. "Let's just deal with business."

"Sounds like you don't want to," she said. I gave her my impressive "Why are you being an idiot?" stare. It's actually not even in a league with my brother's, but it generally does the trick. I started telling her about my morning.

"Why didn't you start with 'Hey, Michelle, someone in a silver pick-up with tinted windows was following me?' rather than avoiding my questions about Digs with lame non-answers?" she asked. "Did you get any other info on the vehicle?"

I closed my eyes and gave her as full a description of the pick-up as I could remember. Silver Chevy pick-up, blue stripe running the length of the bed, windows tinted very dark, probably well beyond the legal limits. Probably Texas plates, but I only said that because when I was in front of the truck in the Denny's parking lot nothing about it drew attention. Out of state plates generally did.

She wrote down the description I gave her and said she'd call Molsby with it, though there wasn't much to go on. There was nothing in the files about anyone's vehicles, and it would be a mistake to presume this was specifically connected to the Hollander case. Still, I couldn't help but think it was. Unless Jeff Veytia had been very obvious about what he was doing, there was almost no way for his potentially wayward employees to be onto us so quickly.

"It could always be someone from a previous case or just a general jerk," I said.

As soon the words left my mouth, I knew they weren't true.

"Just be careful and keep your eyes open, Donovan."

I was forced to agree.

Following that, I gave her the run down on the conversation I had with Mrs. Hollander, and told her about meeting Donna Mahaffey, the previous night's conversations with Laura Field and Digs. She immediately began to get the same vibe I did about Roger Hollander.

"I've known some real creeps and so far he doesn't measure up," Michelle said. "But even if he's a huge creep, he didn't deserve to be murdered. On the other hand, if he was some sort of malevolent neo-maxi-zoom-dweebie, that could at least give us a motive."

I nodded my agreement.

"Where do you want to push a bit more?"

"I think some of the women who worked with him. See what you can find out on Lisa Jefferson for starters," I said.

Michelle said she would. I stood up and headed for the door.

"Where are you going?"

"It's been a busy morning. I need some lunch."

"Tell everyone at Taco Bueno I said 'hi,'" she said.

CHAPTER 22

I went to the drive through at Taco Bueno, got my order, and swung around to the parking lot. I pulled into a space, put the car in park, turned it off but left it so the radio would still play. Clicking through my playlist, I settled on the Dave Brubeck Quartet's *Time Out*. More than 60 years old, the album still sent my mind racing.

The beef burrito was good and the Dr. Pepper was ice cold, the way it tasted best. The music dissected the confusion swirling around this case. Deliberately, consciously letting go of Mrs. Hollander, Roger Hollander, Molsby, Ginger Baker, Michelle and everything and everyone else concerning the case was becoming more and more imperative. The Silver Chevy pick-up with the tinted windows needed to go away for a few minutes, too.

So far the only two people who I thought weren't holding back were Molsby, who gave me literally everything he had on the case, and Mrs. Hollander, who was giving me everything she could think of, but perhaps not everything that there was.

I knew folks who solved crimes by relentlessly focusing on the problem at hand. They got results, so it worked for them. My brain never worked that way, particularly when I got to the point that I could *almost* feel the answers that were just out of reach.

Hitting the gym often helped, but when I needed to relax quickly and more or less keep things moving it was difficult to do better than listening to jazz. Anyone who didn't like Brubeck or Louis Armstrong simply wanted to be a suspect in whatever crime I was investigating at a given moment. Closing my eyes, I leaned my seat back a bit and rolled my head slowly to loosen the muscles in my neck. Without looking, I turned up the volume a little bit.

The first answer that popped into my head was jazz itself, jazz in the form of Kayla Singh, the evening assistant manager at Hollander's Southlake store.

* * *

"She's not scheduled to be in today," Mike McGuckin, the day shift manager at Hollander's Southlake Town Square store told me. One of the younger, way-too-peppy employees had pointed me his way when I asked for Kayla.

I took the opportunity to hit him with the same sort of basic questions I had asked the other store employees. He said he had enjoyed a cordial relationship with Roger Hollander, loved his job, and had never detected any hint of anything inappropriate between Hollander and the company's female employees.

He didn't seem thick or evasive, just genuinely unaware of the stories surrounding Lisa Jefferson. And just like everyone else, he couldn't think of a single reason that anyone would want to harm his late boss, much less kill him in such a brutal fashion. He seemed to have really thought about the subject.

"There's all sorts of people in this world and we all hurt for one reason or another," McGuckin said. "I went through a bunch of jobs and a couple wives before I figured out that you have to find whatever or whoever makes you happy and then actually allow it or them to make you happy. Most people never get there, but then again most people aren't so wounded that they could do something like this to another person."

I couldn't do anything but agree.

"And yet someone did this to Roger, and from the sound of it, it was a pretty ferocious attack. Have you considered that it just could have been someone on drugs looking for more drugs or money?"

"Why do you say that?" I asked.

"Had a nephew. Well, have a nephew, but it's not like I ever get to see him. Got hopped up on drugs. Punched out a cop, then a cop car, then two more cops. Just about bled to death from the cuts on his arms before they shot him. He has no memory of attacking them, but it was all on video. It was like he didn't feel anything. Now he can barely use his arms and suffers blackouts. Pretty much just sits in his cell," he said.

I sort of shrugged.

"What I'm saying is that he wasn't that bad a kid, but drugs can make people genuinely crazy. They can do and endure some seriously scary stuff while they're under the influence," he said.

I was more convinced than ever that what happened to Roger Hollander was a savage, deeply personal reaction to something else. I nodded and made some scribbles on my notepad. Just to make him happy, at first. Then I thought about how convinced I was that I was right, and made a few more serious notes to force me to consider other opinions on the subject.

After I thanked him for his help, I turned to go.

"Hey, do you like jazz?" he called after me.

"Sure. Why?"

"Kayla left me a couple of tickets for the show she's playing in Ft. Worth tonight. I was going to go, but apparently some pipes burst in our church and I have to go help with the clean-up when I get out of here," he said. "The tickets are yours if you want 'em."

I took the tickets.

Vision Convoy, located near Sundance Square in downtown Ft. Worth, was the best place in the DFW area for live jazz. The name of a band, Those Meddling Kids, was on the tickets. I didn't know if that was her group or not, but now I knew what I was doing that evening.

I called Digs to see if she was interested in going, but I got her answering machine and I didn't have her cell phone number. I didn't leave a message, and instead hung up and called Michelle.

"Can I put a new dress on my expense report?"

"No."

"New shoes?"

"Maybe a couple of drinks," I offered.

"Jeez, I'm a cheap date," she said. "What time?"

CHAPTER 23

I found a parking garage just a few minutes' walk from Sundance Square and Vision Convoy.

"What do you think we're going to get out of seeing..." Michelle stopped and looked at her ticket, "... Those Meddling Kids?"

"No idea," I said.

"Then why are we going?"

"Because Kayla Singh is in the band, I'd like to see her again and ask her a few more questions. And because while Vision Convoy might occasionally book acts that I don't care for, they've never hit me with one that I absolutely hated."

She conceded the point.

We walked up to the front doors of the place. The doorman wore an angry face and an expensive suit. He was all attitude for anyone passing by. When he saw us, though, he smiled, checked our tickets and motioned us inside.

"Enjoy the show, Mr. Bay," he said.

I thanked him and promised we'd do our part.

"How often do you come here that the doorman knows you?" Michelle asked.

"Enough?" I said. "I guess it's enough."

Once inside we were greeted by Tina, a South Korean-born, St. Louis-raised history graduate student who was getting her Master's degree at Texas Christian University in Ft. Worth.

"How are you, Mr. Bay?" she asked. Michelle shot me her you-know-everybody-don't-you look.

The lobby had red brick interior walls and a series of floor-to-ceiling windows that in the day would let in more light than would be healthy for a jazz club. Once out of the lobby, though, everything changed.

Black walls and occasional decorative white draperies with black sashes served as counter beats to smooth, artful, and even ornately designed neon lights on the walls. The overhead lighting was kept low and soft, and the tables all had candles on them.

We exchanged pleasantries with Tina as she brought us to our table. The place seated 250 easily and it was mostly full. We were at one of the tables closest to the stage, but we were far enough back that we weren't right on top of them. It was a table I would have picked if I had been picking.

Those Meddling Kids came on stage at about 9:30 and immediately launched into an instrumental version of "St. Louis Blues" followed by an unusual, almost up tempo arrangement of "I've Got You Under My Skin." By the time they hit their smokey rendition of "Round Midnight" eight songs later, I wondered why they weren't on a major label (if there even was still such a thing as a "major label").

The pianist sang lead on most of the vocal numbers, but

Kayla had done an impressive job on "Round Midnight." She went back to her drum kit and two songs later got the spotlight in their version of Paul Desmond's "Take Five," which he wrote as a member of The Dave Brubeck Quartet. Known for saxophone melody and fast piano accompaniment, it has long been a showcase for drummers. And many of them haven't been up to the task, but she clearly was. Seriously, if "Take Five" doesn't elevate your pulse and fire up a creative spark in your brain, there is something wrong with you.

As we sat and watched, Michelle leaned over and whispered in my ear.

"And she sells cell phones for a living?"

I mouthed the words "I know, right?" to her and kept watching the show.

* * *

The band wound down and took a break around 11 p.m. Michelle headed to the lady's room (or as she put it, "the line that dreams of one day actually reaching the lady's room") while I headed to the bar.

Vision Convoy was one of those places that had an extensive, pretentious list of its beer offerings, so I asked for an Old Düsseldorf in a long neck. Because no one *ever* had it in stock. The bartender, who had been quite confident a moment before, now was not, and he flipped through the leather binder quickly.

"I don't think we have that one, sir," he finally said, defeated.

"Oh," I said dejectedly. And by "dejectedly" I meant "happily but acting as if I was dejected." I tilted my head and looked at him to silently further express my disappointment.

He squirmed. I relented.

"Sam Adams," I said. I refrained from asking for the wrong season's specialty Sam Adams and just went with the original.

"We have that!" he chirped.

"I'll have a glass of champagne," a voice almost beside me said. I turned to find Kayla Singh standing there.

"How are you, Mr. Bay?" she stretched out her hand to shake mine. "I take it you and your date somehow ended up with the tickets I left for Mike McGuckin?"

"Pipes burst at his church and he was going to help clean up," I said. "I've never been so thankful for bad plumbing. You guys are really something. How long have you been playing together?"

"Tony – he's on bass – and I have been in several bands together since my junior year in high school. That's why we're so tight. Natalie, on piano player, sort of got the three of us together late in my first year at North Texas. She's amazing," she said.

She motioned to the guitar player as he walked across the room with a chatty blonde on his arm. He did a good impression of a guy appearing to pay attention.

"Guitar George there, he's only been with us about a year. As much as he clearly enjoys the whole being-a-musician scene, particularly the blondes, he's pretty amazing, too. I've seen him walk out of one our sessions and then sit in with a blue grass group," she said.

She pointed out the sax player and talked about how

amazing he was, too. I gathered this might not be her first glass of champagne this evening. I listened to her chat on about the band for another couple of minutes.

"You left out the part about you being moderately amazing yourself," I said.

She laughed.

"I sort of am," she said. "It's weird. I don't feel like an amazing person. I'm not one. But I am sort of good at this and it's stupid to pretend otherwise."

As I was agreeing, she got a sign from the stage manager.

"I have to be back up there in a few minutes. Are you and your date going to stick around for the second set?"

"She's my partner, actually, and I don't know."

She reached out and touched my arm. "You should stay," she said. So I stayed.

CHAPTER 24

"What?" asked Michelle when she got back to the table.

I looked at her like I didn't know what she was talking about.

"You cannot have met a woman in that short a time – oh, wait, I was in line for the ladies's room. You could have met a woman and become engaged in that time," she said.

"You seem pretty sure of yourself."

"One: I'm more sensitive than you about these sorts of things. Two: You may be good at poker, but I emerged from multiple sessions of strip poker not only victorious but losing only my shoes. And three, and most importantly, you didn't get me my drink."

"I could have bluffed my way out of this except for the drink. That threw me," I said.

"See, that's where you say, 'They didn't have the wine you wanted and I didn't think you drank Merlot,' or something like that, Donovan."

"You've done this sort of thing too much," I said.

"That's brilliant, Holmes. How ever did you figure it out?" she said in a bad English accent.

I shrugged.

"And don't shrug at me. Tell me what's going on." I could tell she was scanning the rest of the audience to figure out who might have caught my attention. I didn't say anything, but I could see when it hit her. She slowly turned her head to face the stage and back to me.

She mouthed the word "Really?"

I shrugged again.

"I told you, don't shrug at me. My daddy told me never to trust a guy who shrugged and I'm afraid it's just something that has stuck with me."

"Okay," I shrugged.

"You're an idiot."

"Yeah, well, this just in," I said.

"So, you're going to hang out with little Miss Indian Percussionist who's like 15 years younger than me and beautiful and can sing…"

I nodded, but I didn't shrug.

"And she's… what's that word I'm looking for? Oh, yeah, a witness! That's it," she whispered loudly. "A witness."

"I will be careful. I just get the vibe that there's something more to her story than I know already."

"I know what vibe you're getting. You've seen too many damn Bond movies."

I didn't protest, but I did give her a "you-know-this-is-about-the-job" kind of look.

"And what about Digs?"

"I'm serious. This is work."

"And what about Digs?" she asked again, as if for the first time.

"Michelle, this is really about work, but if it wasn't, we both know that I'm way more into Digs than she is into me. It's one of life's cruel ironies. Or something like that," I said.

She just stared at me for a moment, then shook her head.

"I'll take an Uber home," she said.

"I'll call you later," I said, kissing her on the cheek.

"Watch yourself," she said, then turned around and walked out as the band began warming up for the second set.

* * *

The second set was almost as good as the first. They ran through a string of jazz standards, some of them spot-on covers of the originals, others inventively interpreted. Toward the end of the set, I noticed that Kayla looked a little out of it. She didn't miss a bit, but by the end it seemed like she might have been going on muscle memory. Made sense. Working full time to be able to afford to pursue a career in music, but still something to check out.

* * *

I was standing by the bar again when Kayla came up behind me and slipped her arm through mine. She was a few inches shorter than me and it was a good fit.

"Billy, I will have another glass of champagne, please!" she waved to the bartender.

I ordered a Dr. Pepper.

"You must be some kind of party animal," she laughed.

"Well, I do have to drive home," I said.

"Oh, shit," she said, suddenly startled. "Sorry, my car's in the shop. Tony was my ride and I just let him leave…"

I saw where this was going. World Class Private

Investigator and all that.

"I can give you a ride home," I offered.

She thanked me and said she'd take me up on that offer. The bartender, Billy, arrived with her champagne and my Dr. Pepper. She knocked it back and asked for another. I took a sip of mine.

"So, what did you think of the show? Did you like it?" she asked.

She slipped her arm around my waist and leaned on my shoulder. I told her I did, and suggested that we could call it a night whenever she was ready. She said she wanted to wait for Natalie, their pianist, to come out. She promised it would just take a moment when she did.

In the meantime, she continued to lean against me and that continued to feel all sorts of okay. Another glass of champagne later – and still no Natalie – it was clear she was holding on to me as much for balance as for anything else. Then the saxophonist came by and told her Natalie had left right after the second set. She just laughed.

"We can go now," she said.

I got her coat and put it around her. It wasn't cold, but it was definitely jacket weather. We walked the short way down the street to the garage where my car was.

"Your car is so cool," she said. "It must be like a hundred years old."

"Just about," I said, though I was beginning to think I was the one that was 100 years old. I helped her into the seat, then buckled her in and closed the door. I walked around the car, got in, and started it up.

She had obviously been drinking during the show as well as after it – *Gosh, really? Musicians chemically altering themselves? That never happens!* – sometime before her fourth glass of champagne in about as many minutes, I had made sure I knew where she lived. That was probably a good thing.

CHAPTER 25

FRIDAY

The Firestone Upper West Side Apartments, a landmark, were pretty cool. They were trendy, but not so trendy as to be unaffordable. The apartments had been formed around an actual old Firestone auto service center, on a much smaller scale but in almost the same Mission Revival style as the old Montgomery Ward building less than a mile down 7th from Kayla's place.

I had never been to the Firestone development, but I knew the Ward store because it was a landmark when I was growing up. It had been built in 1928 to be the tallest building in the state. Having survived a flood in 1940, the big tornado that walloped much of downtown Ft. Worth in 2000, and finally Montgomery Ward's bankruptcy and closure in 2001, that building was now luxury residences and shops, another pretty cool address.

There was a lot of that going on in this part of the city and it was, by and large, a really good thing for the area. The redevelopment had closed one of my favorite hole-in-the-wall Tex-Mex eateries, but it wasn't like we were hurting for more of them.

From the Sundance Square area at that time of night, it's about a five-minute ride or less down Main Street to 6th Street, and down 6th until it runs into 7th cutting diagonally across. From there you just followed it until you were at the corner of West 7th Street and Henderson Street.

During the brief trip, Kayla thanked me about five times for the ride home and twice promised to drive me home once she got her car back from the shop, which would be in two days or a couple of months, depending on which version you believed. I had dealt with enough nasty drunks in my career that someone who was nice after having a few too many didn't bother me in the slightest as long as they weren't behind the wheel.

"Oh, I live here, too!" she said excitedly when we pulled up at her building. She insisted that she could get out of the car on her own. I told her I was sure she could, and said I was just there because she'd been so tired. She leaned on me as we walked toward the stairs and continued as we slowly climbed them.

"I really was tired earlier, but I think I'm waking up a bit now. Did you ever see the movie *Xanadu*?"

I told her I hadn't.

"It's horrible, but I love it. Sort of like fast food."

I murmured my understanding, which was marginal at best. Murmuring, of course, allows the listener to hear what she or he wants to hear while permitting the murmurer to express his or her support or lack thereof without consequence.

"Do you like cheese Danish?" she asked as we arrived at her door.

"Love them. Do you have your key?"

She tilted her head back and laughed as if I had unleashed the killing joke, then suddenly stopped and said, "Sure." She fished it out of her purse and handed it to me. I leaned her gently against the door frame as I unlocked the door and reached in for the lights. Sure, some places don't have light switches by the door, but most do and hers did.

The place was beautiful and nicely kept. I was sure that it took most of her salary, but being just out of college with a trendy address and musical career on the upswing wasn't all bad. I helped her inside and closed the door.

She put her other arm around me and kissed me. It wasn't a sloppy drunk kiss either. It was definitely one of those moments when I wished I had less character than I apparently do.

"That's very nice," I said and kissed her on the forehead. "I would love to try it sometime when you've had a little less to drink."

"What are you? Some kind of prude?" she laughed again, dropped her purse on an end table and dropped herself on the sofa.

I walked into the kitchen to see if she had any water in the fridge. I was in luck. It had an ice maker and water dispenser in the door. After one wrong cabinet, the second one I tried held glasses, so I filled it and brought it to her.

"Look, even though it was only champagne and even though you're clearly not going to remember this, you really should hydrate some before you go to sleep," I said as I handed her the glass.

"You're a very nice man, Donovan Bay."

"I'll be sure to tell my mom," I said as I sat down beside her. She put her head on my shoulder.

"I don't usually drink like that," she said.

I couldn't think of what to say, so I didn't say anything. I looked around the apartment to see what there was to be seen. The furniture was nice looking, including a few top of the line pieces. Probably things her parents purchased before she decided on her life of jazz.

It was almost 3 a.m., but I actually grew somewhat more alert because I was irritated with myself. It really felt like almost everyone in this case knew something more than they were telling me, and it included this beautiful, drunk-sleepy girl next to me with her head on my shoulder.

Until she started tracing her finger up and down the inside of my thigh, I had thought she was falling asleep. If I just sat silently for a bit longer, she'd zonk out, or so it had seemed. I took her hand in mine and looked at her.

"Kayla, you are beautiful, and I don't want you think I'm not interested, but not like this," I said and then kissed her again on the forehead.

She actually looked really dejected.

"Why can't I have a decent relationship? Nothing goes how it should?" she put her head back on my shoulder. She brushed a tear from her eye.

"What do you mean?"

"While I was in high school and college, first my parents never let me date and then I never let myself date. Then once I decided that maybe I could…"

I had about a million questions. I asked none of them.

"It's not like I'm naïve. I had a lot of choices made for me, but it wasn't like I didn't know what was going on. When I had to make them myself, I made the same decisions. And then when I finally thought I was ready, I chose so poorly…"

"Hollander?"

She started crying in earnest and buried her head in my shoulder. I held her tight against me and let her cry.

CHAPTER 26

Once the floodgates opened, the deluge commenced. She talked a bit at first between sobs, but it wasn't really anything understandable. She stopped talking and just cried for a while. I sat with her.

After a bit more, she calmed down and cried quietly. When she stopped, she sat in silence, her head still on my shoulder.

"Thank-you for listening to me," she said after a bit more, her voice raspy.

I tried to think of what to say, but she saved me the trouble. She excused herself to use the bathroom and went into her bedroom. I took the opportunity to stand up, move my shoulder muscles, and walk about a bit. I could hear the toilet flush and then the sound of water running in the sink.

In the kitchen, I found a coffee maker and set it to work. Nothing ever tastes as good as coffee smells – one of life's great disappointments, really – but it was good for waking up or staying up.

When Kayla came back in a few minutes later, she was dressed in a University of North Texas sweatshirt and matching pants. Her hair was pulled back and she was wearing glasses. Her eyes were puffy. She'd washed her face, but understandably looked drained. At first she tried to avoid eye contact with me, so I walked over to her and gave her a strong hug.

We sat down on opposite sides of her small dining table and sipped the coffee.

"Sorry," she said.

"For what? You have nothing to be sorry for."

"I've never told anyone about any of this. For a long time I felt that if I even thought about it that I'd end up like a bowl of Jell-O and never venture outside again," she said. "Or end up crying endlessly to someone I only just met."

"I think you need to talk to someone about it, and I'm a pretty good listener, if I do say so myself," I said.

Once she started talking the details just kept on coming. Everything she had told me before about herself previously, in terms of her background, education and working life, was true. But she had left out a lot of details about Roger Hollander.

She shed a few more tears while she was telling me her story, but even as I took in the facts I was impressed by her sense of composure and attention to detail, the measured and self-aware way in which she delivered it. In my experience, most people can't easily separate the emotion from their experiences enough to dryly relate those experiences, particularly rough ones.

Kayla had started seeing Hollander following his experiences with Lisa Jefferson but before she really had any opinions about them. It started with a couple of dinners, then moved onto more distinctly casual outings. Once to the movies, once to Shakespeare in the Park in Ft. Worth, once to a club in Dallas. Outside of the club, in a parking lot just a block away, in the back of his car, he had raped her.

While it was happening, he talked and acted like he wasn't forcing her, like she was responding in kind instead of being attacked. Even afterward, there was such a disconnect between what he had done and what he was saying that she said she was afraid for her life.

When she tried to get out of the car, though, his words changed instantaneously. He told her that it would always be her word against his. He bragged of his family's connections, their reputation, their track record in the community. Then he told her that maybe they ought to just drive over to her parents' house and tell them they'd been doing it.

"I spent a lot of time wishing I'd taken him up on that offer right then. At the time it horrified me. I had defied them by choosing music over medicine, and I really thought them cutting me off financially was them rejecting me. This would only confirm their worst fears," she said.

"That's what these kinds of bastards rely on, their victims being confused and afraid to talk to someone about it."

"I know that *now*. I've done a lot of reading on the subject. The only virtue my silence had was that I probably kept my father out of prison for killing him," she said.

I smiled. I didn't know what else to do. She told me that it went on for seven months, but only periodically, not all the time, but in almost every occurrence it was a repeat of the first instance, with him acting like it was some sort of loving relationship rather than what it was. And each time it was followed with his threats and intimidation.

The physical side of it ended three years ago.

"But you kept working at his company?"

"And I actually got promoted later, well after it was over."

There are many reasons abused people stay with their abusers. It seemed like that was what she wanted to talk about, but it didn't matter to me. I wasn't there to critique how she should have handled the situation.

"It's okay," she said. She reached out her hands across the table to me. "Ask."

"Why did you stay?"

She shook her head slowly from side to side as she spoke.

"I don't know," she said. "Why I've stayed since he died is sort of like my revenge. I don't know if that makes any sense. I don't care. But for why I stayed while it was going on and after it stopped, nothing makes any sense. I could list a thousand reasons and I could be serious about all of them, but I don't think any of them will truly express what I felt inside about myself, or any of it. I thought about killing him. I thought about killing myself. The aftermath of it pushed me closer to my music, my parents, and God, but that's taken me a long time to figure out."

"That can be good," I said. "So why the drinking tonight?"

She shook her head again.

"The truth is that I haven't been able to even begin to approach a normal relationship since it happened. There's been a couple of guys, a few, but nothing good. You seemed intelligent and nice when we spoke at the store, and then I saw you there tonight… I just keep feeling that if I could get past this with someone for just an evening, maybe I could get past it for good," she said.

"Well, I'm glad you talked to me," I said. I took one of my business cards out of my wallet, got up, and went to the kitchen counter, where I had seen a pen while making the coffee. I wrote a name and number on the back of my card.

"You are more together than most people I know who haven't had such a horrible experience, but *no one* gets past this kind of thing without seriously talking to someone. This is the number of a friend of mine. She will be glad to talk with you confidentially, and she's very good," I said.

"Were you serious about trying it sometime without the alcohol?" she asked.

"Doesn't even have to be without the alcohol. Just without so much of it in such a short time."

She laughed, then she yawned. "I'm really tired," she said.

"You should go to bed. Want me to stick around a bit?"

She stood up, so I did as well.

"I think maybe I'm going to be okay."

"Don't kid yourself that it's that easy."

"I meant tonight."

It was my turn to laugh, and then to yawn. I promised to call her.

She gave me a powerful hug, whispered "thank-you" in my ear, and then closed the door behind me.

The only change in my case was that I was glad Roger Hollander was dead. I still had to figure out who killed him.

CHAPTER 27

By the time I left Kayla's place it was 4:45 a.m., I was exhausted and the kind of wired where you're too tired to go to sleep. In addition to being whacked out sleepy-caffeinated, I was also happy that Kayla had opened up to me, angry that I would never get a chance to confront Roger Hollander about what he had done, and confused about how much of this I would ever report to his mother. More than ever, I was sure that I was on the right track with my line of thought.

Before I pulled out of The Firestone Upper West Side Apartments' parking lot, I shot Laura a text telling her that I would like to meet with her cousin who had dated Hollander. Then I texted Michelle and told her that finding Lisa Jefferson had become priority number one, and Vivian Jenkins was number two.

After that, I left Ginger Baker a message on her Hurst Police Department voice mail asking her if we could meet later. I told her I'd like to get her opinion of Donna Mahaffey at Hollander's headquarters.

Late, late at night or early, early in the morning are great times to get anywhere in the Metroplex. Traffic is minimal and you get the faintest notion of what it was like before the population grew dramatically. It wasn't really like it used to be, but it was almost bliss.

Even though I knew more caffeine would only make things worse, I stopped at a Jack in the Box drive-through to get a Dr. Pepper with extra ice for the ride home. And I got a couple of Breakfast Jacks for the Dr. Pepper to wash down. It was a short drive at this time of night, but I just didn't want to be midway when the "wired" gave way to "Sleep now!" I ate the two sandwiches as I drove. It reminded me of college, eating on the run between school and work.

I was startled when my phone rang. It was Michelle.

"Tell me you are not just getting home from that girl's place," she demanded with a sleepy voice.

"Why are you up?"

"Some asshole just texted me," she said.

"You don't turn your phone off at night?"

"Do you?" she asked.

"Ah, good point. Sorry."

"Great. Now tell me you are not just getting home from that girl's place."

"I'm not home yet, but it's not what you think."

"What I think is that you're a very strange man."

"Oh, then maybe it is what you think. I'll give you the non-details later, but I'm more convinced that someone Roger had treated in reprehensible fashion came back to even the score," I said. "And while I want you to follow-up on the people I texted about, I also wanted you to work on alternate theories. I can feel my thought process becoming pretty committed to my theory, and that might not be a good thing."

"So, you took me to a jazz club, put me in an Uber, and sent me home, took this beautiful – and yeah, I can admit she was hot – and exotic musician home to her place, and nothing happened?"

"Know what's worse?"

"Things were getting serious and you blurted out Eleanor Roosevelt's name in a moment of passion?"

"No, it was your name actually."

"You are a very strange man."

"Yeah, I might have heard that somewhere. Anyhow, the worst part was she was actually hitting on me in no uncertain terms and I was stuck being the good guy. Have I mentioned how I hate that kind of thing?"

She laughed.

"Thanks."

"No, Donovan, while you're developmentally challenged in many ways, I'm glad you are who you are."

I told her that I was going to get some sleep and that I'd be in around lunchtime. She said she'd get working on tracking Lisa Jefferson and Vivian Jenkins, and then she said she was going to try to get a little more sleep and hung up. Two minutes later I pulled into my driveway. Three minutes after that, I remembered to pull my blinds closed. Then I dumped my shirt, pants and socks on the floor, pulled on a clean, well-worn T-shirt, climbed into bed, and turned out the light. It couldn't have been two minutes later that I was asleep.

* * *

At 8:47 a.m. Digs called. I only know that it was that precise time because I looked at the phone later. While it was ringing, I tried to turn off the alarm on my clock radio and eventually yanked its cord out of the wall when it wouldn't stop. Then it dawned on me it was the phone, and I eventually figured out how to answer it.

"You still asleep?"

"Out on a case until about 5:00 this morning. Can I call you later?"

"Sure. I was just returning your call from last night."

"My call?"

"Yeah, you called and didn't leave a message."

"I'll trust you on that," I said. "Bye."

I hung up and dropped the phone on the floor and my head back onto the pillow.

CHAPTER 28

Less than a half hour after Digs called, the neighbor's lawn service started up. For a few minutes I tried to fight it, but their mowers and leaf blowers made it certain that I would get no more sleep that morning. I sat on the edge of the bed for an inordinate amount of time during which I contemplated a ninja-like attack that would leave the lawn service crew strewn about my neighbor's yard, separated from their implements of distraction as well as their heads. Since I was too tired for that, I zombie-walked to the bathroom and turned on the shower. A few minutes later I climbed in, breathed in the steam, and let the exquisitely warm water wash over me. While it wasn't enough to shake the fog, it did wonders for my muscles as I rolled my neck and stretched. After a while, I cooled the water down a bit and tried to actually wake up. It worked a little.

I shaved, got dressed, and called Michelle. "I thought you'd sleep in a bit more," she said without a greeting.

"Me, too."

"I'm going to send the phone to voice mail and concentrate on tracking down those leads for you, so call my cell if you really, really need to talk to me. Otherwise, the more you leave me alone, the faster I will get what you need."

I told her I'd give her a call sometime after lunch to see how it was going, but I'd leave her to her work. She said that would be fine.

"You might want to give Tyler a call to check on him," she said.

I told her I would, and then she said "Ok" and hung up. I dialed Tyler's cell.

"What's up, Mighty D?" he asked.

"People really don't say 'hello' anymore, do they?" I asked.

"I don't know about people," he lied. "What can I do for you, chief?"

"How's it going on the case?"

"Great, but I can't really talk now. Want to meet for lunch?"

"Sure. Call me around noon and we'll figure out where," I said.

He agreed and we hung up. Then I called Digs back.

"Hey, I'm in a meeting. Can I call you back later?" she asked.

"Sure," I said.

"Okay," she said and she clicked off.

Civility was really going all to hell, wasn't it?

I decided to go get some breakfast, so I grabbed my jacket, my car keys, my case folder, a notebook and some pens. It felt like getting ready to go to school and take a test. I figured some caffeine might help and knew it certainly wouldn't hurt.

There are a lot of great restaurants in the Dallas/Fort Worth area, but the Mid Cities were sorely lacking in traditional diners and coffee shops. In fact, they were nearly completely missing in this region. I have nothing against Starbucks or any of the chains, but getting what they serve is not the same as a great plate of scrambled eggs, hash browns and toast to go with your morning brew. There are so many transplanted northerners – try going to a Rangers game or a Stars game and you'll spot the caps from Detroit, New York, Boston and elsewhere – that you'd think someone would open one.

Oh, well. I settled on IHOP in Bedford. Sally Gayle, who was the hostess, the assistant manager, and ran the cash register, smiled when she saw me. I always doubted she remembered my name, but she knew my face. She sat me right away in my usual spot and told me that Dorothy, my waitress today, would be right with me. I knew Molsby would be happy that it was a waitress and not a "dude waitress."

I tried not to laugh out loud, but was chuckling anyhow when Dorothy walked up to take my order. She wasn't looking up as she walked, but when she did and saw me she stopped and pulled out her order pad.

"Quick two-egg breakfast, eggs scrambled, wheat toast, bacon, and a Dr. Pepper?"

I nodded yes.

"What's so funny?" she asked.

"That I'm so predictable," I said.

"Hmmph," she said, turned on her heels and walked back to where she entered the order. I never had figured out why I wasn't one of her favorites, not that I ever really had tried. But it was a little odd that she seemed to look down on people who came to the International House of Pancakes since she, in fact, worked at IHOP. I shrugged to an audience of no one and got out my notebook to start writing down everything from the night before.

Dorothy returned with my Dr. Pepper. I nodded my thanks, but kept on writing. There had been so much that I quickly decided I had to actually do a full Roman numeral outline, which made today even more like a school day.

I was scribbling furiously when Dorothy returned with my meal. Without much comment, she set it down nicely in front of me, fished in the pocket of her apron for a small bottle of Tabasco sauce, and set it down as well.

"Thanks," I said. She managed a semi-pleasant grunt and walked off. People were all sorts of amusing, but at least the food was tasty. I continued writing as I ate, so it took me a while. The place wasn't as busy as it might have been, so no one but Dorothy seemed to mind that I was taking so long. I switched from Dr. Pepper to hot tea and kept working.

I was finally beginning to actually feel awake. And even though I now had all sorts of ideas about Roger Hollander, the case was no less confusing.

CHAPTER 29

While I was sipping hot tea, I continued making my notes about the case thus far and specifically about Roger Hollander's modus operandi with Kayla. No one who does that kind of thing does that kind of thing only once. The phone rang. It was Laura.

"You were out late," she said.

"Really? No one says hello anymore?"

"Hello," she said.

"I appreciate the gesture."

"So, hello, you were up late last night. Were you out on a date?"

"It was related to the case," I said.

"That's not a denial, Donovan."

"If you want the short version, no, it was not a date."

"But there's a long and complicated version in which the conclusion is somewhat more murky?"

"You say that like you're asking a question, but it comes out more like a statement," I said. "Why is that?"

"Because we've known each other a really long time," she said. "And we have a history."

"Point taken. Did you get a hold of your cousin?"

"Yes, I did," she said. "Now listen, before I go any further with this, my cousin –her name's Sandy – is a very private person. She was sort of the family wild child before my sister came along and stole that crown, but now she's the kind, wise type that everyone goes to privately for advice. Tread gently," she said.

I promised to do so and reminded her that she knew she could count on me.

"I know. I know. I just had to say it," she said. "I'll text you her address. She's only working a half day today, so you should be able to catch her at home after lunchtime."

"Thanks, Laura. I'll let you know how it goes," I said.

"You won't need to. I'll hear about it."

As soon as I finished the call with Laura, I motioned to Dorothy for the check. She brought it over with all the grace and attentiveness of a bureaucrat under investigation by a special prosecutor. I cursed myself for leaving a decent tip, then I paid up and headed to the car.

* * *

Digs called back just as I was getting in the car. She apologized for not being able to talk earlier while she was in her meeting.

"Hey, can I ask you a blunt question?" I asked.

"Sure. Shoot."

"You'd tell me if there was anything more I should know about your relationship with Hollander, right? I don't mean lurid details. I mean, if he'd ever put you in a position you didn't want to be in…"

"Donovan, I can't think of a girl the age I was then who hasn't had to deal with some guy's pushy behavior or things like that," she said. "It was over when I ended it. That's it."

"Okay," I said.

"What made you ask about that?"

"The more I find out about the guy in recent years, the more I don't like," I said.

"Wow. I don't know, but just... wow," she said.

I didn't know what else to say. The silence just hung there for a moment.

"But, hey, to awkwardly change the subject, what are you doing this evening?" she asked.

I told her I didn't have plans. She invited me over for dinner. Nothing special, she said, she just felt like cooking. She told me to come by around 7 p.m. and I told her I would.

What I didn't tell her was that I really wanted to know that Hollander hadn't pulled the same number on her. I didn't want to think I could have missed something like that, but I knew that with my feelings for her then I could have been oblivious to it. I was relieved to hear what she said and thought she could very well be right about him escalating the behavior. I looked forward to talking with the ladies Michelle was trying to track down for me and with Laura's cousin, Sandy.

* * *

"Max Norman and Bebe Ally are guilty as sin," Tyler Newsup said as he bit into a slice of wheat toast. We were at Denny's again because it was close to ESC Key Comics and on the way to Norman and Ally's apartment, which he had been staking out quite a bit.

"I have a friend who has a big deal comic book shop in Baltimore, buys a fair number of high-end back issues, sells a bunch. At any rate, I had him post comments on a site they frequent implying that he was looking for high grade copies of the comics in question," he said.

"Did they take the bait?"

"I'm sure they think they were being very subtle. My friend is going to be here for a convention this coming weekend, and they messaged him that they have a client who wishes to remain anonymous but who might be interested in selling said high grade copies," he said.

"And?"

"And they want to meet with him during the show," he said.

"Okay. Well, keep me posted."

Tyler assured me he would as he spread grape jelly on another piece of toast.

* * *

"I can't believe you actually left me alone to actually allow me to do actual research that you actually asked me to actually do," Michelle said as soon as I answered.

"I occasionally listen," I said.

"Well, I've got addresses for both of them and some other information. When are you going to be back at the office?"

"I'm in Euless. I can head there now," I said.

Unlike Digs, Lisa Jefferson and Vivian Jenkins had known Roger Hollander in recent years. If this guy had escalated his behavior, maybe they knew of others he had preyed upon.

CHAPTER 30

Michelle had made up folders with her research on Lisa Jefferson and Vivian Jenkins. My phone pinged as I walked through the door and I noted that she had just sent me the same information via email as well.

"Good timing," she said.

"Had to happen sooner or later. Law of averages and all that?"

"Probably," she said, but she was shaking her head "no."

She gave me her thoughts on both women, sticking only to the facts. I listened as I read through the information. It was all very basic stuff, but the most important information – physical addresses, email addresses, telephone and cell phone numbers – were there.

After she finished, I filled her in about my conversation with Laura and my impending conversation with her cousin, Sandy. She listened and took down a few notes of her own. Following that run down, I related my conversation with Tyler about the Jeff Veytia case.

She nodded a bit as she wrote.

"When are you seeing Laura's cousin?"

"As soon as we're done here."

"Do you want me to talk to either Jefferson or Jenkins? We don't have a lot else going on."

"Check with Tyler. Make sure he doesn't need any back-up. If he's okay, why not start with Lisa Jefferson? Keep me in the loop, but it's entirely your call," I said.

* * *

I had never had a witness or contact ask me to meet them at a church before. I once had a congregation as a client – it took me all of three days to find out who was stealing the copper wiring from the huge external air conditioning units at one of the big Baptist churches – but that was about it. Sandy Schulz was the first.

When I had called her, she said she was working at a re-sale shop affiliated with a large Methodist church in Bedford. She said she volunteered there and that when I arrived we'd be able to walk over to the church itself and speak privately.

Tyler would have immediately noted that her surname was spelled the same as Charles Schulz, the late creator of *Peanuts*, and not the more familiar Schultz.

Despite hearing of her for many years, I had only met her once before, and it was at the funeral of another of Laura's cousins the summer after we graduated high school. So in other words, a million years ago.

I parked by the shop and Sandy was the one who greeted me when I went inside. She was one of those people who immediately puts you at ease, even if you were just meeting them for the first time. A blonde with long straight hair pulled into a ponytail, she wore an oversized sweater over faded blue jeans with cowboy (cowgirl?) boots.

"Rebecca, I'm going to walk over to the church," she yelled to the back of the store.

"Okay! Thanks!" Rebecca, unseen except for a waving arm, said from behind a rack of clothing.

"The things we sell are donations, and we use the money we raise to help people who have run into bumps. It's not a lot of money, but we help with things like utility bills or medicine or what have you," she said as soon as we stepped outside.

"Sounds worthwhile," I said.

"It's mostly retirees who work here, but there's a few of us slightly younger folks, too."

"Does it really work or is it just to make the people donating feel good?" I asked.

"A fair question. The answer is you wouldn't believe how many people we've helped. Most of them have just been hit by an unexpected bill or their unemployment benefits haven't kicked in. Some are worse off, but there are just a lot of people on the edge."

We reached a doorway on the main church building. She very casually paused and waited for me to hold it for her, which I did, and we went inside. It was nice, clean, and clearly well cared for. It was neither heavily traditional nor thoroughly modern, but it was most definitely church-like, which only seemed appropriate.

The sanctuary was at the far end of the long, carpeted hallway.

"Pastor said we're welcome to talk in here," she said. We entered the sanctuary, which actually leaned more toward the modern than the traditional, and took seats with one between us on the last row of pews.

"When Laura called and told me that someone wanted to talk to me about Roger Hollander, it really surprised me. Of course I had heard on the news about his murder, but I hadn't seen him in many years," she said. She was seated on the end of the pew and was turned to her left, facing me. She stretched out her left arm along the back of her seat and the one between us.

"There's a lot about that time in my life that I'm not very proud of. Laura might have told you that between the cousins, I was the proverbial wild child," she said, smiling.

"I know her sister," I smiled back.

"Ah, my successor to the family title, bless her heart. Kimberly marches to the beat of her own drummer, doesn't she? Well, I'm no one to give up on someone else who is so clearly lost. He didn't give up on me when I was there," she nodded toward the large cross, "so what right do I have to give up on my own family?"

"Knowing Kimberly, I bet you've been tempted."

She laughed a hearty laugh and rolled her eyes.

"Seriously, you may know her casually, but you have *no* idea," she said, wiping tears from her eyes. "But you came here to talk about Roger Hollander and me, so let's do that."

CHAPTER 31

"I started dating Roger Hollander the summer before my freshman year," Sandy Schulz said "He was about to start his senior year. He was good looking, popular, and a football player. And most importantly to me, he chose me over my older sister, Cynthia, who was everything I wasn't."

She spoke in measured tones at a deliberate pace. She didn't fidget or get overly emotional. Her eyes closed occasionally as she searched for the right words.

"Cynthia was beautiful. In truth, she was elegant in a way teenagers almost never are. She was popular, socially active, and already had a promising future ahead of her. And worse, she was actually nice," she said with a smile.

"I was awkward, into punk music, and dressed accordingly. I distinctly did not feel beautiful or attractive or lovable. My parents loved me, but they certainly didn't know what to make of me. Cynthia in many ways was the child parents wish for. My younger sister, Ramona, was very much along the same lines, which made me feel even more distant. I started drinking while I was still in junior high school, and that led to experimenting with drugs and with boys," she said.

While I had met her once before, I didn't know her, so I couldn't say for certain that it wasn't a rehearsed performance. My gut, though, said it wasn't.

"Cynthia was a year behind Roger, but they knew a lot of the same people. There was a party at the house of someone else on the football team. I know it wasn't Roger's house, but I can't remember the boy's name. The only way my mother would let my sister go was if she took me along. Now like I said, Cynthia was a good girl, but you can imagine how much she loved that idea," she chuckled.

"Well, I wasn't anymore into being the wet blanket than my sister was to have me along, but she really wanted to go to the party. I was just the price she had to pay, so we went," she said.

"I don't think there was ever anything going on with Cynthia and Roger, but I remember pretty clearly that she liked him a lot and was very flirty with him. He sort of played it back to her a little bit, enough to encourage her to keep it up, but that's about it. But unlike any of the other older guys at the party, he actually treated me like I was there," she said.

She paused and looked at me, trying to read me.

"I know this must seem like a lot of really unnecessary information and I'm sure you have a lot questions you'd like to ask," she said.

"You're doing fine," I said.

"My husband knows the broad strokes, but not the details. My therapist knows the whole story, but I've actually never told it to anyone else, so I'm sorry if I'm rambling."

"You're not rambling at all. You're giving it context,

which I really appreciate. Please continue."

She closed her eyes and kept going.

"Roger and some of the other guys had a few beers and the party was tame by today's standards, but for us back then it seemed pretty wild. At any rate, Cynthia was off talking to some of her friends. I went to use the bathroom. When I came out, Roger was there in the hallway and no one else was around. He told me he was really glad my sister brought me to the party. I tried to be cool, but my heart was pounding. I said I was glad she brought me, too. He brushed his hand on my cheek, then looked me in the eyes and asked if he could kiss me," she said.

She opened her eyes and met my gaze. "That was about the last time he asked permission for anything when I knew him," she said.

"I felt like I might explode or dissolve into nothing if he didn't kiss me. And when he did kiss me, it was like being instantly inducted into a secret society, a group with only two members. I couldn't tell my sister because she really liked him, and he said it would just be our secret," she said. "Time and experience being what they've been, now when someone talks to me about secrets, my first instinct is to shine a light on what they're saying. At the time, though, I just didn't think that way."

The rest of the story was stunning in its similarity to what Kayla had confessed. He had raped her while acting like it was consensual. He had effectively blackmailed her into continuing a relationship with him to keep him from telling her sister and her family about her behavior.

To compensate, she began drinking even more, taking drugs, and in general engaging in self-destructive behavior. Her grades began to suffer, so her parents got her a tutor. Her health began to be affected, so they took her to the doctor. She began acting out toward them, so they got her a therapist. When her parents urged her to dress even just a little bit more femininely, she got a tattoo.

"One night, in the back of his pick-up truck, he was starting his usual business with me. He ripped open my blouse and pulled up my skirt, and he saw the tattoo, and it was like a switch had been thrown. He told me that I disgusted him and that I should get dressed. I did. Without another word, he drove me home, dropped me off, and never called me again," she said.

"Never?"

"Not a word. For me, the damage to my self-esteem had been done and I had several years of self-destructive behavior ahead of me, but through clearer eyes I look back and think that tattoo might have saved my life."

"What do you think happened?"

"My therapist told me that in Roger's twisted mind I wasn't pure anymore, or something along those lines. Of course it was never going to make any sense in a rational way, but inside his brain it meant cutting me off," she said. She told me that opening up to faith had brought her back from the edge and turned her into the person that she was today.

I told her that I really appreciated her talking to me about it, and asked if she would mind if I followed up with her if I thought of something else.

"I'd rather not keep talking about it," she said, "but if it will help you put some closure to his death, I'll do it. I am glad about where life has taken me, and it couldn't have done so without me forgiving Roger Hollander. I didn't get any happiness from knowing that he'd been killed."

It was more clear than ever that Hollander had picked victims he was sure wouldn't talk. It was a shame that Sandy Schulz hadn't ever talked to someone in law enforcement about it – there had to have been many women since she suffered at his hands – but I wasn't about to get into his victims sharing his blame.

I thanked her again and showed myself out of the church. As I walked back toward my car, I thought about this guy and whatever demons had driven him. I didn't look forward to the notion that I was going to have to ask Digs about him again tonight, now we had a clear pattern of behavior.

I had an increasing certainty about why he was killed.

Now all we had to do was find out who he had pushed far enough that they did something for all his victims.

CHAPTER 32

I called Ginger Baker at the Hurst Police Department and asked if she had time for a cup of coffee. She said I could swing by the station or she could grab lunch and I could meet her at Sutherland's. I chose Sutherland's and told her I'd meet her there in 15 minutes. As I made my way from Bedford to Hurst down Harwood Road, I thought about the conversation ahead.

We'd come up with a strong theory with lots of supporting circumstantial evidence, but nothing iron clad. Roger Hollander's pattern with women should at least have shown up before we got involved. Why hadn't it?

The ability to take in the case as a whole rather than building it piece by piece could be a huge factor. It was also the one area in which the passage of time was more of a benefit than a hindrance. It was months after their investigation had cooled, but not so long that the players had forgotten the details. And more importantly, I had their whole case file before I ever really started working.

While there wasn't even a single homicide per year on average in Hurst, there were plenty of other crimes to investigate and there were only so many officers to go around. As excuses go, it's not a good one, but it's unfortunately very realistic.

In my mind, those were their only two outs. I wondered why we'd been able to uncover all of this in a week.

* * *

Detective Baker walked into Sutherland's about two minutes after I arrived. Being a world class private investigator, I immediately noticed that she was wearing a skirt instead of a pants suit as she was the first time I met her. It worked for her.

"Court appearance this morning?" I asked.

"What?" she was startled for just a moment. "Oh, yeah. The Burkhart case. It was swell." Which I supposed translated to it was routine, boring nonsense.

The hostess showed us to our seats, our waiter arrived, and we ordered in pleasingly quick succession.

"So how's the Hollander case going?" she asked.

"That's what I wanted to talk with you about. It seems pretty clear that Roger Hollander had an M.O. for abusive relationships dating as far back as high school. You guys didn't get any hint of that?"

"No. Not at all," she said. Surprise showed on her face. "We didn't get a whiff of anything like that. How did you get onto it?"

"He graduated four years ahead of me at Bell. We knew some of the same people, I went from there. But I got the start from a couple of his female employees."

She sank back in her chair.

"This was my first big case here. I can't believe I blew it

so badly," she said. She looked for a solution to the problem on her shoes. I doubted it was there.

"Hey, these are just leads. Nothing but a M.O. and a possible motive. If we come up with anything concrete, it's yours, but I just wanted to keep you in the loop and see if you'd thought of anything else."

The waiter arrived with our drinks as well as our food. Over her cheeseburger and fries and my soup and salad, I gave her my view of things without hanging anyone who had spoken to me confidentially out to dry. If it turned out later that I was right, I'd have to share more information with the authorities, but right then I just tried to paint the picture as I saw it. We had a pretty good motive, but we had no suspect. We almost certainly didn't know all of the women Roger Hollander had seen over the years, any one of whom could be our killer.

Baker looked like I'd let the air out of her tires. I didn't want to tell her that she shouldn't feel that way, but I stressed that I had the easier job with no other crimes demanding attention and no bosses talking about my outstanding open cases. She seemed to appreciate my comments.

"You'll keep me up to speed on this?" she asked as she got up from the table.

"I wouldn't say anything to anyone up the food chain yet," I said.

"Sure thing. Thanks," she said.

* * *

As soon as I got back in the car, my cell phone rang. It was Tyler Newsup.

"Are you or Michelle or both of you available tomorrow

night?" he asked as soon as I answered.

"Michelle should be. I might be. What's up?"

"I've got a meeting set between my Baltimore comic book dealer friend and our ambitious couple," he said.

"Good work. When and where?"

He gave me the details. I jotted them down and promised to get back to him as soon as possible. Right now I was operating on little sleep, so I liked the idea of letting Michelle and Tyler handle it. But I also knew that I could use anything with some closure right about now, so I'd go if I could swing it.

While I was waiting on my dinner with Digs and for Michelle's report on the Lisa Jefferson interview, I decided to head home and get some sleep. If I could get an hour or two, I'd be in a lot better shape this evening and it would increase the odds of tagging along on Tyler's bust.

It only took a few minutes to get from Sutherland's to my place. I figured it would take me a while to fall asleep, but I stretched out on the sofa and turned on the TV for some background noise. Then I was out like a light.

CHAPTER 33

It's rare, but there are times open warfare next door wouldn't wake me. Normally, though, just about anything could pop me out of sleep, no matter how tired I was. So, the single tone from Michelle's text was enough.

I looked at the phone. Not bad. I slept more than two hours. Michelle's text was simple: Check your email.

There was a message from her with a Word document attached. I clicked to open it. It was headlined "Report on Lisa Jefferson."

After our discussion this morning, I headed to Arlington to ascertain whether the Lisa Jefferson residing at 2311 Balsalm was indeed the same Lisa Jefferson who worked at the Southlake Town Square for seven months at Roger Hollander's store there.

I arrived there at approximately 10:45 a.m. and was able to locate her condo in just a few minutes. I rang the bell and Ms. Jefferson answered the door. I introduced myself and asked for a few moments of her time. She asked what it was regarding. I told her we were looking into the murder of Roger Hollander.

She appeared shocked at the mention of his name, almost literally staggered. I asked if I could come in, and I ended up helping her to the sofa. She was shaken. Once she was seated, I went to the kitchen area and got her a glass of water. After another few moments, she caught her breath.

Upon somewhat regaining her composure, she asked if I thought she killed him. I told her that we were just trying to get background information on Mr. Hollander and that some preliminary investigation had yielded some indications about his personal life on which we wanted to follow-up.

Not knowing Ms. Jefferson previously, I did not have a baseline of her personal demeanor to which to compare her state at that point, but as an experienced investigator and observer of people, it is my belief that she was rattled or disoriented. I did my best to calm her down and bring her back to the subject of my visit, gaining background on Mr. Hollander, specifically regarding her employment with his company and their relationship.

She was at first very hesitant to disclose any information and eventually admitted this was because of the non-disclosure agreement signed as part of her settlement with Hollander's firm. I told her that no NDA can compel her to violate the law by withholding information from a murder investigation. I told her that I could not compel her testimony, but that the authorities could, and that if she didn't talk with me she would more than likely end up talking with them.

This again upset her, but I was able to calm her down by assuring her that it was not our intention to make any of this public, and that I would do my best to see that she was kept out of the entire matter.

The basic picture was along the lines of what you ascertained previously. Age 22, estranged from her parents in San Antonio and working her way through University of Texas at Arlington, she was hired as a frontline employee at the Southlake Town Square store. After initially resisting Mr. Hollander's advances – which he seemed to take good naturedly – she was promoted to Assistant Manager and she began working more closely with him. She soon acquiesced to his attentions and they went out on several dates.

Ms. Jefferson said after going out four times and things seeming very good between them, the fifth time they went out Mr. Hollander physically detained and raped her. She said that during the rape he continued to talk to her as if everything was fine, as if it was consensual. Afterward he took her home, again acted as if everything was fine, and gave her a warning that if she breathed a word of it or in any way acted differently, that he would give her more of the same or worse. Then he politely dropped her off at home, once again acting as if it had been a normal date.

She told me that she did not initially seek medical attention after the incident.

The relationship with Mr. Hollander continued at times of his choosing for two more months. It stopped abruptly, she said, when she became pregnant.

Ms. Jefferson reported that the physical assaults stopped immediately. I asked if that was what resulted in the settlement. She said yes, it had.

She went to a drawer in her kitchen and returned with

several photos of the child, a boy, named Reynold Jefferson. He lives with her parents in San Antonio. Aside from the child, she said her relationship with her parents was repaired because of the ordeal, and that he is being raised in a good home.

At this point, she seemed much more relaxed, so I broached the subject of her whereabouts at the time of the murder. She again went to the counter drawer, pulled out a file folder, returned to the sofa and handed it to me. It contained the paperwork of her voluntary committal to a private psychiatric hospital in New Braunfels, Texas. Admission and release dates will have to be confirmed, but according to the information she provided she was under in-patient treatment at the facility.

I thanked her for talking with me about what I was sure was a very difficult subject. I asked her if she knew of any other women who might have been the subject of similar attentions from Mr. Hollander. She said she did not, but while she was in therapy she came to understand that it was likely there were others, that such attackers did not do what they did to only one victim.

The thought of this appeared to deeply distress Ms. Jefferson. After crying for a few moments, she excused herself and again went to the kitchen. She opened another drawer, pulled out a pistol and shot herself in the head.

I immediately called 9-1-1 and attempted to attend to her wounds. She had no pulse. Arlington police arrived in three minutes and EMTs arrived approximately two minutes after that. She was declared dead at the scene.

While they were attending to Ms. Jefferson, I texted Sgt.

Molsby and asked him to put in a call to anyone he knew at Arlington PD in terms of my character and credentials in hopes of keeping this under wraps to the extent that it relates to our investigation.

I dialed Michelle's phone immediately. It went to voice mail. I left her a message that I was on my way to Arlington. I grabbed my jacket, a ball cap, and my keys and headed for the door. I didn't know the street, so I would use GPS to find it. I closed the door behind me, then stopped. I knew I had probably locked the door behind me, but couldn't remember doing so. I checked and I had done it. I got in the car, started it up, spoke the street name in Arlington into the GPS on my phone and headed to find Michelle.

* * *

Michelle called about five minutes later.

"Donovan, it was... It was the most horrible thing I've ever experienced," she said. "

"I'm on my way. GPS says I'll be there in 15 minutes. Are you okay?"

"No, I'm a mess, but yes, I'm okay," she said.

"How did you ever put together such a quick report after something like that?"

"I knew I was going to start shaking uncontrollably as soon as it really hit me, and I can barely hold the phone right now, so I did as much as I could as fast as I could. I have a voice transcription app on my phone, and I knew it would be my best chance to get things down accurately."

"But you're okay?"

"I'm okay, Donovan, but would you just hurry up and get here?"

"Who's the lead from Arlington PD?"

"Detective named Tanner. I don't know him."

"Charlie Tanner's a good enough guy. I know him. I'll be there as soon as I can." I hung up and drove faster.

CHAPTER 34

There were three Arlington Police Department cruisers and one unmarked car in the parking lot. I spotted Michelle's car and then her standing beside a couple uniformed officers.

In addition to being a good investigator and organizational queen of our office, Michelle's a tough cookie. She put her arms around me and dissolved into sobs as soon as I arrived on the scene, but she recovered quickly.

Charlie Tanner saw me and came walking over.

"Okay if I put her in my car?" I asked him.

"Sure. She gave us a very detailed statement. Really kept her head about her. Very impressive," Tanner said.

I nodded and told him I'd be right back. I walked Michelle over to my car and opened the passenger door for her. She got in. I told her I'd be right back after I talked to Tanner.

"Nice to see you, Donovan. Sorry it's over something like this," Tanner said.

"Same here, Charlie. Could you keep our names out of this as far as the press are concerned?"

"It'll get out sooner or later," he said.

"I know. Just until it does," I said.

He agreed.

"What's this about? Off the record."

"The Roger Hollander murder last year. Maybe. I don't know anymore."

* * *

I took Michelle home. As soon as I dropped her off, I called our mutual friend Suzie Sinclair, the counselor who I had recommended to Kayla. I let Suzie know the basics of what had happened and asked her to pay a visit to Michelle at her earliest convenience. She said she would.

* * *

I didn't want to work on this case anymore. I didn't want to hear one more horrible story or learn one more detestable fact about Roger Hollander. I sat in the car for a few minutes after talking with Suzie and thought about whether I could continue or not without it just being for the money, which I'll admit we definitely needed with or without the case that Tyler was working.

Roger Hollander didn't hire us. His mother did, and she deserved answers, even if they turned out to be ones she didn't like. And although I was a firm believer in capital punishment, I didn't think it should be meted out by anyone other than the proper authorities. No one deserved to die how he did.

I set the phone down, started the car, and backed out of the space. I dropped it into gear and pulled out of the parking lot. Normally I would have just hit the highways and driven around a bit to shake the emotions flooding my head. Instead I took to the back roads. They weren't as back roads-ish as they were years ago, but I knew a few areas that still weren't overly crowded.

If I was going to be able to think about the case in any useful fashion – and if I was going to be able to enjoy my dinner with Digs at all – I had to shake some of this loose from my head. I cranked the radio and kept driving.

* * *

Digs was in the kitchen cooking up a storm when I arrived. She managed to stop long enough to let me in, but then she was right back at it. It looked like she was having a good time, which was nice to see. The kitchen had family photos on the walls, including one that obviously came from a few years back with Digs, her sister, Juliet, better known as Jules, and Rhonda together. They all looked happy.

Sometime in the last five years Digs had transformed from the girl I knew, who could probably have burned water, to the beautiful, passionate cook entirely at home in the kitchen, eager to share cooking tips and offer tastes and smells of things in progress.

I mainly just sat on the bar stool at the kitchen counter and watched. For the old Digs "try this" was more along the lines of "Does this smell bad to you?" but now it was an invitation to share her enthusiasm.

When I got to know Digs and Jules, I had never met a more dissimilar pair of identical twins. The same was still true. If you didn't know them, they were very difficult to tell apart. They had certain traits, mannerisms and speech patterns in common, but they dressed differently, exhibited different sensibilities.

In high school, Digs didn't really know what she wanted

to do with her life. Jules was on the rifle team and wanted to be a U.S. Army sniper even though at the time the Army didn't even offer sniper training to women. Their father had been a sniper and their older brother was in Special Forces.

After graduation, their careers followed those tracks. Digs wandered from job to job in search of a career, while Jules enlisted in the Army the day after graduation. Despite not knowing what she wanted to do, Digs generally seemed if not happy then certainly okay, while Jules furiously butted her head against the Army's glass ceiling.

Years later, Digs found a calling as an emergency medical technician, which led to her being recruited by a major company that manufactured and sold fire equipment all around the world. As it turned out, it seemed to be the job that was made for her.

Over that same span, Jules stayed in the Army, went to college, went to Officer Candidate School, became a military police officer, and had unintentionally (or so she said) seen combat in Iraq and Afghanistan. I didn't expect her to get out after a mere 20 years either. How much of Juliet's passion for military life came from her hero worship of their dad and their late brother, I never knew, but it really didn't seem that odd.

I was one of the chosen few who were friends with both. Though I was closer to Digs, I initially had more of a thing for whichever one I spent more time with. Eventually that ended up being Digs because there was only so much time I could spend at the target range and not look like a chump while Jules talked it up with the experienced, older shooters.

Digs and I had never actually dated. We had served as

each other's "plus one" any number of times, and we'd gone through our phases, but that was about it. There were points at which I thought I'd explode if something didn't happen, but nothing happened and I did not, in fact, explode.

But it was always this thing in the back of my mind. Finally, five years ago, neither of us were dating anyone and we had gone to dinner. Over some truly disappointing barbeque – that really should have been a sign to me; you can't throw a rock without hitting good barbeque in Texas – I told Digs exactly what I had been thinking.

The scene was sort of like that *Farside* cartoon where the goofy guy frets over whether the woman loves him or not and the woman's thought balloon shows her thinking something like "I like yellow." Digs not only shot me down, she was stunned I had even thought that way.

We made a few faint-hearted efforts to hang out after that, but it was definitely awkward. I figured if we were going to survive it as friends it would take a while, so I left her alone with the idea she'd call me when she was ready.

And then five years passed.

"Hey, you've been sort of silent. What are you thinking about?" she said.

"The ancient past," I said.

"Oh, that," she said and laughed. "Let's concentrate on the here and now."

CHAPTER 35

With a bit of a flourish, Digs set in front of me a beautifully presented plate of what she described as Thai cucumber salad. While the main ingredient was clearly cucumbers, I could distinctly taste cilantro and lime juice in addition to the peanuts, which were easy enough to spot. I also guessed crushed red pepper, but missed on the basil. Still, she was at least a little impressed.

"Look at you, knowing ingredients! When did that happen?" she laughed. She was clearly enjoying herself.

"Man cannot live by Taco Bueno alone," I said.

"Who are you and what have you done with the real Donovan Bay?" she asked.

For the second course, she served Spaghetti Carbonara. If I had a weakness beyond Tex-Mex, it was bacon. It was accompanied by two sides I would not have picked but which worked well together, corn and broccoli.

She served it with a 2011 Keller Dalsheimer Hubacker Grosses Gewachs Riesling, again not something I would have expected. She saw me eyeing the label.

"I have several very nice reds if you don't like this, but

I've been on a bit of a Riesling kick for the last few months and for reasons I can't quite explain I think it goes great with the Spaghetti Carbonara," she said.

Even though I generally don't like "fruity" wines like some Rieslings, I had to admit it was a decidedly bold, successful choice.

"When did you get so good at this stuff?" I asked.

She told me that she had decided to take a cooking class five years or so ago, and that led to a wine-tasting trip to Napa, followed by more cooking classes, and joining a wine club.

"I'll never be a wine snob because regardless of what anyone says, I just like what I like," she said, "but I usually have at least a few good bottles on hand. I really enjoy discovering good new ones and introducing my friends to them."

"Well, here's to new discoveries with old friends," I clinked my glass into hers.

She finished the dinner with a slice of apple pie, a small scoop of cinnamon ice cream, and cup of tea. All in all, the best meal I had enjoyed in ages. Elegant presentation, great taste combinations, and perfect portion sizes.

After we finished, we moved to the living room. I sat on the sofa.

"That was a fantastic dinner, Digs. It's like you're a grown up or something," I said. She plopped down right beside me.

"It's really nice to get to hang out with you, Donovan. I've missed you so much and I'm so sorry how I handled things back when," she said. She put her head on my shoulder and I almost instantly, simultaneously loved and hated the fact that it felt like it had always belonged there.

"I think you said it right earlier. We should just concentrate on the here and now," I said.

"Okay," she said. "How's the case going?"

"I thought you didn't want to talk about it."

"I was a little freaked out. Now it's just weird."

"I'm making some headway. We have a few more people to talk to, but the more I find out the more I think you were very lucky with this guy. He was a genuine, Grade A creep."

"But you want to ask me just one more time if I really was so lucky," she said.

"Yeah, I do. He…" I paused for a moment because I really wanted to gauge her reaction while I still possessed some shred of objectivity. "It seems like he really hurt some of these women."

"Donovan," she put her hands on my face and gently turned my head to look directly at her. She met my gaze. Her eyes were as piercing and as beautiful as I had ever seen them. Here was a woman, a friend, I needed to start seeing in grown-up terms and not through the nostalgic lens of teen angst.

"For whatever reason, Roger was only a jerk to me, nothing worse. Even though you're only mentioning it in the vaguest of terms, I don't want to spend a lot of time thinking about how I got lucky. I just want to be thankful he didn't hurt me," she said.

"You're sure?"

"I think I'd know."

"Okay," I said.

"Now, though, I want to finish what I was saying earlier, about how I acted when you told me how you felt about me…"

"Listen, Digs, it took a while, but we survived it," I smiled at her, then looked down at my shoes, hoping I'd written some notes there. I hadn't.

"I lied. I knew how you felt. I always knew how you felt. I never said anything about it because you never said anything about it and I didn't want to lose you as a friend, and…"

She grew silent.

"And?"

"And your timing sucked," she said. "I didn't know then what I know now."

"What's that?"

She suddenly swung herself around, straddling me, so she was facing me, her arms around my neck, looking me straight in the eye again.

And then she kissed me.

And I kissed her.

After a few minutes, she stopped just as suddenly and pulled back just a bit.

"What? Donovan Bay with nothing to say?"

"Oh, I have a lot to say," I said. I stood up with her still wrapped around me. She laughed and kissed me some more. With one arm around her, I turned off the light. We didn't hurry.

It had taken more than half of my life and I wasn't about to rush it now.

CHAPTER 36

SATURDAY

I once again forgot to close the blinds and I was once again awakened by the bright rays of the sun in my eyes. Only this time it wasn't my fault because it wasn't my room, and I didn't mind in the slightest anyway.

Like every clichéd romantic movie I'd ever seen, I didn't move; I just watched Digs as she slept. The sensation was more overpowering than anything I could have imagined.

I propped myself up on one elbow and kept watching. A few sounds filtered in from the outside. A mocking bird a couple of yards over. A car slowing down at the stop sign and then accelerating. But it was otherwise almost still. It seemed appropriate to be contemplative. I tried to breathe quieter.

The single tone my phone let out to signal a text message from Michelle seemed way, way too loud, even though the phone was tucked in the back pocket of my jeans, which were in a pile of clothes on the floor. I slowly shifted on the bed and began reaching toward my pants, which seemed to be just beyond my ability to stretch. I shifted again, then stopped to see if I had disturbed Digs – no change – before again trying to make my arm extend further than it possibly could.

My index finger caught part of the waistband and I pulled it closer to me to a point where I could actually grab the jeans. My belt buckle scraped the floor slightly, another noise that seemed way louder than it should have, but I was able to lift them to me and slowly slide back almost into my original position. I extracted my phone and silently lowered the jeans to the floor.

"After yesterday, I'm going to let you interview Vivian Jenkins. Thanks for calling Suzie. She's going to come over this morning. How did things go with Digs? Don't forget Tyler's going to try to close the deal this evening. – M."

I switched the phone to silent mode and began texting Michelle back with one hand while keeping myself balanced next to Digs with my other elbow.

"Take the evening off. I will cover things with Tyler. Will talk to Vivian Jenkins on Monday," I replied to her.

The phone vibrated quietly in my hand almost immediately.

"You're still with her, aren't you?"

"I will talk to you later," I replied.

"That's a YES! Happy for any good news," she sent back.

"Please tell me you aren't texting with another woman while I'm actually in bed with you," Digs said. Her eyes were still shut.

I went with the truth.

"It's Michelle, about one of our cases," I said.

"Did you tell her where you were?" she asked, smiling.

"I neither confirmed nor denied," I said.

Her eyes popped open. She rolled over and looked at me.

"A non-denial is a confirmation," she said.

"She sort of said the same thing," I admitted.

Digs rolled back onto her back and closed her eyes again.

"Anything ever happen between you and Michelle?"

"No."

"Ever think about something happening between you and Michelle?" she asked.

"Yes," I said.

"And...?"

"And that's all," I said.

"Good answers," she said and smiled.

I kissed her on the forehead.

"I don't want to get ahead of things. I'll tell her to keep it quiet," I said.

"Donovan, I don't care about that. I've got a lot of baggage. I'm sure you have baggage. Everyone has baggage. But even five years later, I *know* you."

I smiled. I didn't know what else to do.

"What?"

I kissed her.

After a moment, she stopped.

"Two things. One, is this worth waiting just a few minutes more for?" She flung the covers down and then back up.

"Definitely," I said.

"Good, because I have to brush my teeth. I know it's not all romantic or anything, but I can't stand the way my mouth is in the morning," she bolted to her feet, grabbed a t-shirt, and dashed into the bathroom with a laugh.

"Do you have a spare toothbrush?" I called after her. I

heard the water turn on, then off just as quickly. She stuck her head back out.

"If I say yes, would you kindly just accept that my mother made sure that I am always prepared for visitors and not the sort of person who does this all of the time?"

"Seems fair enough," I said.

"Then yes, I do have a spare toothbrush for you," she closed the door and I heard the water come on again. After a few minutes, she came out wearing the t-shirt. It was just long enough as long as she was perfectly still, which she wasn't.

"My turn," I said and headed for the bathroom.

When I returned, Digs was sitting up with her pillows stacked behind her.

"We got sidetracked. What was your second question?" I asked.

"We've known each other forever, but there are things we've never talked about before," she said. "So I have a really important question for you."

"Shoot," I said.

"Are you like every other guy who wants to see his women in sexy, highly impractical, frequently uncomfortable lingerie of questionable functionality?"

"Oh, not at all," I lied.

"Because I was thinking of getting some," she said.

I laughed and kissed her again. She responded in kind.

CHAPTER 37

Late that morning, after we woke up again, Digs caught me staring off into space. I had been thinking about Lisa Jefferson and how troubled she must have been and wondering why the hell Michelle had to be there when it happened. I was glad Suzie was stopping by her place. I knew Suzie would follow-up with me, but that didn't make the event itself any less horrible.

"What are you thinking about?" Digs asked.

"Things for which there are no answers. A case Michelle was working on. She saw something yesterday no one should ever have to see. I sent a therapist friend of mine to see her this morning, and in the long run she'll be fine, but I hate being the guy who sent her there," I said. "It's not something you can ever un-see."

She snuggled in next to me and I put my arm around her.

"Sounds unpleasant. Want to talk about?" I smiled.

"Thanks, but no. I'd rather keep that business away from..." – I motioned to her, me, around the room – "all this and just what we have right here right now."

"It is sort of nice, isn't it?" she asked, her hand rubbing

my chest slowly.

"More than a little," I said.

I must have grown silent again, but this time I was apparently grinning as I stared off into space.

"What?" she said.

"What *what*?" I asked.

"You're doing it again. And you weren't thinking about that case because you were smiling."

"And here I thought I was the detective."

"Spill the beans."

I rolled onto my side and looked at her face to face.

"We've had, oh, a spectacular night and an equally wonderful morning. We've survived the whole teeth-brushing question and another woman texting me while I was in bed with you. That's a lot for a first date," I said.

"But…"

"Relationships have stages. I don't want to take anything for granted, and I really don't want to screw something up because I'm too comfortable with you too soon," I said.

"I'm with you so far."

"Good. Is it too soon for me to ask you to take a shower with me?"

She burst out laughing.

"I had no idea where you were going with that," she said and gently slapped me on the chest with the palm of her hand.

"Well?"

"I think that sounds like a scary idea. Let's do it," she said.

I jumped to my feet and scooped her up into my arms

before she could move. She squealed like a teenager.

"Donovan, you'll hurt yourself!" she laughed again.

I lowered her and she put her feet down on the bathroom tile. She pressed up against me and we embraced and kissed. She turned on the water.

"Oh, and now will come that whole awkward preferred water temperature discussion that ruins so many relationships," she said.

"Perfect," I said.

* * *

It was one of those things. I had loved Digs in one way or another for half of my life, but now that things were finally happening I really didn't want to go overboard with expectations or demands on time that we weren't ready for... even if I didn't know what they might be.

We sat on the sofa, eating a pizza and drinking Dr. Pepper. She was wearing a different, slightly longer T-shirt that proclaimed "6 out of 7 dwarfs are not Happy." I had my jeans and shirt on because, well, that's what I had with me when I got there.

"There are really criminals who steal comic books? Like comic book comic books?" Digs asked.

"Yep. And apparently I'm going to help Tyler bring them to justice this evening. He's set up a buy with some high profile dealer friend of his from Baltimore who is in town for some convention."

"Will it be dangerous?"

"They're idiots, so of course there's some chance of danger. We'll do all of our preparation to limit the number of things that could go wrong. Tyler's an experienced operative. I've been doing this a while. And we'll probably have a couple of undercover officers there as well," I said.

"And these comics are worth hundreds of dollars?"

"Hundreds of thousands of dollars."

"I'm in the wrong business," she said.

"You and me both, Digs."

She was quiet for a moment, then looked at me funny.

"What?"

"Do you think it's going to be very late when you're done?"

"Maybe late, but not very late. Maybe around 10 p.m.," I said.

"You should come back afterward," she said.

I didn't argue.

* * *

Tyler picked up on the first ring.

"I'm on my way. Michelle's sitting this one out. Where are we doing this?"

"My friend Josh Geppi, my high-end comic book dealer from Baltimore, has a hotel room in Dallas near the convention center. I have us set up with another room there, and the two friends on the force I mentioned are ready to join us," he said.

"Great. Text me the hotel info and I'll meet you there."

"Will do. See you soon," he said and hung up.

CHAPTER 38

Tyler wanted me to time my arrival in Dallas so that I'd be at the hotel just before the convention let out for the day. He and his friend, Josh, would meet me in a suite set up to look like what I imagined would be typical quarters for a high end dealer at a convention, whatever that might be. Those were details for Tyler and Josh, and I knew from experience that Tyler knew how to make a suspect feel comfortable. Given the general traffic situation in the Metroplex, I surprised myself by arriving more than 20 minutes early.

The hotel, The Hayes Suites, was immediately across the street from the convention center and connected to it by a pedestrian walkway on the third floor. I handed the keys to my car to the valet along with a tip healthy enough to get and keep his attention. I told him that I didn't know how long I'd be, anywhere from a few minutes to a few hours, but I wanted it close by and yet relatively safe. He looked at the car, then back at me, and smiled.

"No problem, boss," he said. "She's a beauty and she'll stay that way."

It was my turn to smile.

I walked in the front door and into the main lobby. The place was pretty posh in the way so many convention center hotels aren't. It was beautiful, functional and well maintained. The front desk was straight ahead. To the right of it were banks of elevators, to the left was a restaurant. There was also a waiting area with seats and various decorative plants. There were two temporary signs welcoming guests from both the comic book convention and a rodeo promoters convention. I couldn't see those crowds mixing a whole lot, but if I had any spare time it might have been fun to watch.

A beautiful blonde with a name tag that read Ylette at the front desk asked if she could help me. I told her most people thought I was beyond help, but she could certainly try. The way she smiled let me know she didn't get the joke, but that was okay. I gave her my name and she gave me a large manila envelope with my name written on the front.

I opened the envelope. It was a copy of Frank Miller's *Sin City*, the hardboiled crime graphic novel that had inspired the movie. On the back of one of his business cards, Tyler had written "Use this for cover." He was pretty funny at times. I smiled, tucked the card into my pocket, and tossed the envelope in the nearest trash can. I texted Tyler and let him know I was there and took a seat in the lobby while I waited for his answer.

His reply came a bit later, just as the protagonist, Marv, was breaking into his parole officer Lucile's place for his medication. I closed the book and looked at my phone.

"Room 1518, 5 minutes," the text said. I kept reading for two minutes, then closed the book again and walked to the elevators. One going to floors 15 and higher dinged open before I even finished reaching for the call button. I got on and pushed the button for 15. I reached the room about less than half a minute before Tyler and his friend.

Tyler introduced me to Josh. He was a solid-looking guy with a good handshake and a ready smile. He looked like he could take care of himself if things got dicey. It was our job to make sure they didn't, but also to be prepared in case they did.

"I have two friends from the Dallas Police Department on the way. They should be here in less than 10 minutes," Tyler said as he slid his key card in the door lock. "I emailed them a copy of the theft report from Euless, and I have a copy with me."

He opened the door for us. Josh went in first, followed by me, and Tyler closed the door after us. The suite was a nice one. Tyler had already set the main room up with some clothes in the closet, shoes on the floor, and multiple boxes of comic books from his own collection. He even added touches ranging from Japanese mecha models and a two-foot high Godzilla on the dresser to assorted wrappers into the garbage cans and a couple of half- consumed beverages on the end tables.

"Officer Jack Miller will play Josh's assistant. He knows just enough comics to be dangerous, but he's a good guy and can pull this off," Tyler said. "He's bringing Detective Tony Regent with him."

He pointed to the doorway into the suite's main bedroom.

"Tony and I will be in there. And you'll be in the second bedroom on the other side," which he then indicated. Both rooms have monitors hooked into video feed from these cameras. He went over to the Japanese mecha models and the Godzilla and pointed out the small camera lenses in each.

"You're too much, Tyler," Josh said and shook his head.

"Hey, listen, I hope these ass-clowns haven't thought this out any more than I think they have, but we're talking at least $500,000 worth of comics here. With that kind of money on the line, it pays to be prepared," Tyler said.

There was a knock at the door. I moved toward the room I was supposed to hide in. Tyler looked through the peephole and motioned me to stop. He opened the door and let Officer Miller and Detective Regent into the room. They shook hands with Tyler and did the casual wave to Josh and me as Tyler introduced us.

Tyler ran through the same plan with them and then it was time. Detective Regent and Tyler went into the main bedroom. I was in the second bedroom. Tyler's set-up with the monitor worked well. I could see Josh as he flexed his hands open and closed and exhaled deliberately, shifting slightly in place to stay loose.

Then there was a sharp knock at the door.

CHAPTER 39

Officer Miller opened the door. "Can I help you?" he said.

"We're here to see Josh. We have an appointment," said a male voice trying desperately to sound calm and authoritative.

"Oh, sure, c'mon in," Miller said.

Max Norman and Bebe Ally entered the room dressed in the costumes they had worn to the comic convention. Max was supposed to be Indiana Jones, if Indy was about 5'4" and had a bit of a pot belly. Bebe was one of the Sailor Moon characters, don't ask me which. She was about 5'6" with shiny, long, straight black hair.

I had never seen them before, but it was immediately clear which one of them wore the figurative pants. To be fair, if I looked like Max, Bebe could have told me what to do, too. The fancy leather briefcase Max carried looked ridiculously out of place.

"I'm Josh," Josh said and stepped forward. He shook hands with Max and then with Bebe. "Jack, why don't you grab a couple of those chairs in the dining area and bring them over here by the coffee table.

Although it hadn't been part of the script, it seemed natural enough and Officer Miller just rolled with it. He placed them on one side of the coffee table with the sofa on the opposite side. First Bebe sat down and then Max did. Max kept the briefcase close to him, right beside the chair.

"You guys have a good day at the show?" Josh asked.

They said they had, but they were clearly nervous and wanted to get down to business.

"I picked up some great books, but I'm really looking forward to seeing if what you have is as good as you described. If it is, the money we agreed upon is no problem. I have a cashier's check for you right here," he patted the left pocket on his shirt.

"$250,000, right?" Max asked. Josh nodded.

Max seemed satisfied. He looked to Bebe, who nodded affirmatively to him. He reached down, picked up the briefcase, and placed it on the coffee table. He slid the lock and I could even hear the solid click sounds in my room with door closed. He opened the case, lid toward Josh. Even on the video I could see the subtle shift in Officer Miller's bearing until Max pulled out the 9.2 copy of *Amazing Fantasy* #15 and the 9.4 copy of *Tales of Suspense* #39.

Max closed the lid of the briefcase again, but did not push it firmly closed. I knew Miller was watching it in case he had a weapon in there, and so was I.

Once they've been certified, comic books, like stamps, coins and numerous other collectibles, are encapsulated in clear, hard plastic cases that surround and protect the issue. They also have a label that indicates title, issue number, date of publication and other notable information. The *Amazing*

Fantasy #15 noted "First appearance of Spider-Man," and the *Tales of Suspense* #39 likewise listed "First appearance of Iron Man." Both belonged to a recognized pedigree collection, so they each also carried the description "Paris, Texas Collection" on the labels as well.

"Whoa, just look at these beauties," Josh said and let out a small whistle of appreciation. He set them down gently on the coffee table and smiled beamingly, like a man very comfortable with what he was about to purchase.

"Beautiful," he said. He pulled out a magnifying glass and began to inspect them.

Bebe glared at Max.

"I thought you didn't have to do that if they were independently graded," Max said, a bit nervous.

Josh stopped and looked up at him.

"Son, if you have someone else willing to pay $250,000 without taking a look, take the deal. Otherwise, I'm taking a look," Josh said. He let it hang there, kept his gaze on Max and waited for a reply.

As soon as Max said, "Okay," Josh's gaze went back to the comics. On the monitor in the side room, I saw the large and easy-to-read serial numbers that had been given to the two comic books on the labels. The magnifying glass was a camera, one of Tyler's tools. The numbers were, no surprise, exact matches to the stolen comics, not that there were other copies of the same issues in the Paris, Texas Collection, or so Tyler told us.

"Well, I'd say we have a deal here, folks. I'm pleased to present you with a cashier's check for $250,000," Josh stood up, pulled the check from his pocket, straightened it out, and held it out to Max. "We do have a deal, right?"

"Oh, yes, sir, we have a deal," said Max, accepting the check. Bebe was beaming. I'm almost certain she knew how she was going to spend every penny.

"Max Norman and Bebe Ally, you are under arrest for the theft of these comic books and their illegal sale," said Detective Regent as he and Tyler came through their doorway into the main area. "Place your hands on the backs of your necks and do not move!"

Detective Regent had a good cop voice, but Max still went for the gun he had in the briefcase. Officer Miller slammed the top of the briefcase with his fist as Max reached in.

"My hand!" Max screamed, staggered backward and fell to the floor. Miller moved to step around the table toward him and that created a moment in which Bebe saw only one way to stop everything from slipping away.

She went for the gun and had her hand on it before she felt my gun against the base of her neck.

"Please don't," I said.

The officers placed both of them on the floor, cuffed them with their hands behind their backs, and searched them.

"Nice work," Detective Regent said to us.

I thanked them both and Tyler patted Josh on the back.

I pulled out my cell phone and called Jeff Veytia to tell him that as soon as the legal proceedings were done – and probably a lot sooner – he'd have his comic books back.

Josh asked if he could talk to Mr. Veytia. I handed him the phone and he immediately started trying to buy the issues in earnest.

Tyler had to pack up his stuff, both his tools of the trade and the props from his collection, but he was basking in how cool Josh thought it was to be involved in the sting.

"We're gonna grab some dinner and beers," Tyler said. "Want to hang out a bit?"

"Normally, yes, but I've barely slept in two days," I said. Oh, and I had Digs waiting for me, but he didn't need to know that.

"Next time," he said and shook my hand. "Thanks, as always for the work, chief."

CHAPTER 40

The valet saw me coming, motioned me to wait just a minute, and ran off to get my car. True to his word, he was back in under a minute. The tip I gave him when I arrived would more than have covered it, but it had been a good night and I gave him another.

I got into the car, put on my seatbelt, closed the door, put it in gear and headed back toward the Mid Cities. I was glad this case was wrapped up because the Hollander case was just a big fat pile of pestilent goo. There was just no way this was going to end well. If I was right, the trail was going to lead to someone Roger Hollander had physically and mentally abused, someone who finally snapped and killed him in gruesome fashion. It was going to be someone I couldn't blame, even if I couldn't excuse it.

And with what Michelle had been through yesterday, we were doing nothing but paying bills and our salaries now while adding therapy to her list of expenses for the foreseeable future. I picked up my cell phone to call Mrs. Hollander and tell her we were quitting the case, but instead I called Michelle's number. She answered after three rings.

"Hey there," she said. She sounded tired, but not asleep.

"Did I wake you?"

"Oh, no, but I did take something that Suzie prescribed and I am actually pretty relaxed. The downside was no wine," she said.

"You'll always be able to whine to me, sweetheart," I said.

"I want more money," she said.

"See, my point exactly. How are you doing?"

"Pretty messed up, but I suppose I'm going to be okay. How'd it go with the great comic book caper?"

"They're busted and everyone's fine. I'll give you all the details later. Just wanted to let you know it was wrapped up."

"Good. Good," she said. And then she was quiet for a bit. "Donovan, thanks for having Suzie come over today. That was really thoughtful and it really helped, at least a little bit."

"Good," I said.

"Would you mind taking me to church tomorrow morning? Suzie said not to drive while I'm taking these pills."

"Do I have to do all that Catholic stuff?"

"You're a very strange man. You know that, right?"

"Which service?"

"10 a.m."

"No problem. I'll see you about 9:45 Good night, Michelle."

I hung up and concentrated on the drive. Traffic was remarkably light and even with the construction I was making good time, so my concentration lasted about ten minutes and then I began thinking more intently about Digs. Which in turn made me drive a little faster.

I called her and let her know I was on the way. She suggested ordering a pizza and I didn't argue. She called it in so it would be there when I got there. Even with all the crap that infused this case, I was smiling as I drove. And that was so ridiculous it made me smile more.

* * *

My phone rang. It was Laura.

"What are you in the middle of, Donovan?"

"Driving back from Dallas…? And we're back to not saying 'hello,' I take it?"

"Hello, Donovan, and I by that mean, I just talked to Michelle. What the hell is with this case?"

"I don't know. I wish you could tell me. I'm going to take tomorrow off and leave the whole mess alone and see if any more pieces fit into place on Monday," I said.

"Okay. Well, if you need anything else you know where I am," she said.

"Thanks."

"And, really, Digs? It's like high school all over again. Teen angst, notes in study hall, hot and cold running hormones…"

"Thank-you, Laura. Gotta go now."

She laughed and hung up. I dropped the phone on the passenger seat and kept driving.

* * *

I pulled up out front of Digs' place about 10 minutes later. I've always been at least a little bit self-aware, so the extra bounce in my step amused me, not that I tried to suppress it or anything. I was about to knock on the door when she opened it. She was wearing a simple t-shirt and jeans, a combination she had always made look good.

"So, are we now safe from the big Texas Comic Book Crime Wave, or can we expect more to come?" she asked.

"Oh, I think we're safe for the time being," I said.

"Good!" she put her arms around my neck and kissed me. I grabbed her, picked her up and carried her to the sofa. She almost screamed with laughter. I kissed her again once I put her down on the sofa.

"Not that I don't like where this is going, but the pizza guy ought to be here in a few minutes," she said.

"You can spend time with him later," I said and kissed her some more.

"You know what I mean," she said after a couple more minutes.

"Yeah, okay," I mock protested. I sat up just as the doorbell rang.

* * *

"Can I make an observation without sounding like I'm already an old fogey?" Digs asked after we had eaten a few slices of pizza and moved to the bedroom.

"Sure," I said. We were in bed, sitting up with pillows propped behind us, watching TV.

"Just a few years ago, this would not have been true, so that's why the age reference," she said.

"Okay," I nodded.

"My brain wants to fool around right now, but my stomach says we better wait."

"I totally get that. I have to admit that in just about every other respect I'm feeling like I was much younger, but yeah, I get what you're saying," I said.

"It's not very romantic," she said.

"But it's better than belching or worse at an inappropriate time. *That's* not very romantic," I said.

She leaned in closer to me, I put my arm around her, and we watched a re-run of *Monk* until she fell asleep. I woke her up later just so she could brush her teeth, of course.

CHAPTER 41

SUNDAY

I woke up as the earliest wisps of sunlight crackled across the horizon. Pondering the imponderable – why was I up when I was tired enough to sleep until the following day? – I looked over at Digs and laughed quietly at myself.

I was in the middle of the worst case I could think of – I hated the *victim* – and simultaneously was involved with a woman I adored since I was a teenager. "Wow," I said silently.

Even though it was a lost cause, I closed my eyes and tried to go back to sleep. I started thinking about Roger Hollander and the women he'd hurt. Lisa Jefferson may have pulled the trigger, but Hollander loaded the gun for her. I decided I wasn't going to spend my day thinking about this. In fact, I was going to spend my day thinking about all the good stuff.

Like I've said, sometimes how I solve things is letting them be back burner items. Think about other things or don't think much at all, then revisit the problem, and you can end up seeing it very differently.

* * *

Digs was up, showered and dressed and had decided she

was coming with me to take Michelle to church. I finished getting dressed. We decided to take her car since someone would have had to ride in the back of the Mustang and none of us were toddlers. She had a recent model, four-door, black Hyundai Genesis. As we walked out, I headed toward the passenger side, but she tossed me the keys. I must have looked at her funny because she laughed.

"Yeah, I know, it seems so domestic to have the man drive."

"Just as long as I didn't say it."

I opened the passenger door for her and then closed it once she was in. Once I got in and started it up, I adjusted the seat and the mirrors, and then we headed to Michelle's via my place so I could grab a sports coat.

* * *

"You're being too nice. I'm not a flower. I'm not a piece of china. I just need some company," Michelle said as the three of us were walking up to her church, Saint Bernadette's.

"What are you talking about?" I asked.

"Under normal circumstances he refers to my church, which he knows I dearly love, as Our Lady of Eternal Bingo, and that was only after I threatened to kill him if he didn't stop calling it Our Lady of the Evening," she said to Digs. "The fact that he actually used its proper name is not a good sign."

I opened the doors for both of them. Digs gave me a look and I admitted it was true by way of a shrug.

"Oh, thank goodness it's not just me he shrugs at," Michelle said.

We sat through the service without saying much, Digs on

one side of Michelle and me on the other. My upbringing was a bit too Baptist to ever be really comfortable in a Catholic service, but the priest, Father Juan Gonzales – who looked nothing like the former Texas Rangers slugger – delivered a very good message with a near perfect combination of solemnity, happiness and humor with almost no hellfire or brimstone.

On the way out, Michelle thanked us for bringing her. We offered to take her out for lunch, but she said her dad was going to stop by, so we dropped her off at her place.

"I've got a couple of appointments already scheduled with Suzie, but this really helped," she said as she gave me a big hug. As I was walking back around the car to get in, she gave Digs a thumbs up when she thought I wasn't looking.

* * *

I had brought a few things with me and kept puttering in the kitchen, periodically shooing Digs away so she couldn't really see what I was up to. The remainder of the day was what I needed it to be. Digs and I spent the afternoon watching movies on the sofa and not watching movies in bed.

The Peruvian roasted chicken with a spicy cilantro sauce, the dinner I had been preparing most of the afternoon, turned out to be a hit. I didn't tell her I had only learned how to prepare it recently in my cooking class. Instead, I just smiled and basked in her mystified adulation.

"I wish you didn't have to work tomorrow," she said later that night, under the sheets, lights out, tired, happy, still sweaty.

"So I could stay home while you went to work?"

"Okay, Captain Literal, I wish we both didn't have to work tomorrow."

She ran her hand over my chest as I held her close. We were silent for a few minutes.

"I'm glad this didn't happen sooner. I wasn't ready for it," she said as she put her head on my chest. I stroked her hair and just accepted the moment's perfection for what it was. In the morning the weekend would be over and I would be hip deep in the muck again.

CHAPTER 42

MONDAY

I wanted to stay for breakfast, but I needed to put in a full day and that meant going home for a shower and clean clothes, so I kissed Digs goodbye while she was still in bed and headed to my place. Once there, I cleared the mail from the mailbox, checked my voice mail, rifled the fridge for expired stuff, and set out the garbage at the curb. Then I hit the shower.

Tap water in Hurst is horrible to drink. It's one of the few things I hate about my town. To the touch it's got a soapy quality. It comes from far enough down in the ground that this is a commonly known issue, and it's just not pleasant to drink. But the water pressure, particularly in my shower, is great. I would gladly trade my shower with its superb water pressure in favor of Digs' shower with Digs in it – I'm not a *complete* idiot – but there really was no beating the cascading spray of hot water pulsing down on my back and neck. I rolled my shoulders and neck and loosened up, and I even did some stretching as my muscles relaxed.

After showering and shaving, I got dressed and headed to Michelle's to pick her up since we had left her car outside Lisa Jefferson's place in Arlington. I told her that I was going to drop her off at the office and that her dad and I would go get her car.

"I told you before, I'm not some fragile flower," she said, irritated. "I don't need my daddy to save me from the monster in the closet."

"I know all of that, and you're right," I said as we pulled up outside the office. "But you also don't need to revisit this so soon either, okay?"

She thanked me, closed the door behind her, and headed up the stairs to our office. She was still irritated but by the time she sat down she'd know I was right. I headed over to pick up her father, who didn't live too far away.

Michelle's dad, Dwayne, was a semi-retired gunsmith who mainly traded in antique firearms. Normally chatty, he didn't have much to say, so we made most of the ride to Arlington in silence with only Louis Armstrong to accompany us.

"That woman must have had some powerful horrible troubles, but I don't think much of her passing them on to my daughter," he said as we closed in on Lisa Jefferson's place. I nodded because I didn't think there was anything to add to it.

"Yep," I said.

We turned off the road and into the development and spotted Michelle's car right away. He had the keys out and was ready to go. "I think I'll walk home from the office. I could use it," he said with a wink and patted his belly.

* * *

Vivian Jenkins, now Vivian Bauer, worked for Palmiotti & Gray Realtors in Arlington. The minute I met her I wished

Michelle had come to talk to her and let me talk to Lisa Jefferson. Vivian was young, self-assured, outgoing and pretty. Some of it could have been an act because it was real estate and her job was selling expensive things, but she was very likable.

I introduced myself and she asked me into her private office. It wasn't large, but it was nicely appointed and organized to make the most of the space it had. It was done in warm, friendly colors and I imagined that she closed a fair number of deals in it. I thanked her for seeing me and asked her if she was aware of the circumstances of Roger Hollander's death.

"Of course I heard about it when Roger was killed, but I really haven't thought about my tenure with his company for a long time," she said. "It was an okay job, but it wasn't a career or anything like that. I was just out of high school, newly divorced with a one-year-old, trying to get my legs underneath me and start making my way in the world."

"I understand that you and Mr. Hollander went out briefly."

She smiled a bit awkwardly and tilted her head slightly. "My. You've done your homework," she said.

"Nothing to worry about, Mrs. Bauer, I'll explain further in just a moment."

"Well, yes, we did go out. I think it must have been three or four times. It was very nice and I actually liked him a bit. But even though I was 19 and looked like I was 16, I'd been through the whoopee machine. My high school sweetheart promised to love me forever. I thought having a baby and getting married would be wonderful and then I got figuratively punched in the face and thrown in the woodchipper by reality. So when things looked like they might take a serious turn with Roger, I made sure he met my little boy, Henry," she said.

"How'd that go?"

"On the surface, it was great. Instead of going out to dinner, I invited him over so I could cook for him. I don't know how he didn't know I had a child – it was on all my employment forms – but he didn't. I could tell it was a big surprise to him. He actually did great with Henry, but on his face, his countenance, it was like someone flipped a switch. It was over," she said.

"How did he treat you after that?"

"He was a total gentleman. Always asked how Henry was doing, things like that, but that was it," she said. "Does that help?"

"It actually confuses things more," I smiled, "but I'm very glad to hear that's how things went."

She looked at me as if she was trying to look right into my brain. Her smile faded a bit and a bit of the street-smart skeptic showed up.

"Mr. Bay, what is it you're not telling me?"

"It's not my place to speak ill of the dead, Mrs. Bauer, but Mr. Hollander's relationships did not always end so well."

She seemed to consider this for a moment, then the smile returned. We both stood up.

"It's funny, but after that time with Roger, I did the same thing anytime I thought a guy might be thinking about getting serious. The only one who stuck around after I introduced them to Henry turned out to be the love of my life, his stepdad," she motioned to a picture of her husband and her son.

"A great looking family, Mrs. Bauer. Thanks for your time," I said.

On the way to my car, I pulled out my cell phone and called Suzie Sinclair. Her assistant said she was with a patient. I asked her to have Suzie call me back and told her it would only take a couple of minutes.

I hit the road and headed back toward the office.

CHAPTER 43

Once I was in the car and on the road, I called Ginger Baker at the Hurst Police Department. I asked if she had time to grab some coffee and follow-up on the case. She told me that she could meet me at Donut Wheel. I was silent for a moment.

"Sue me. I like donuts and coffee," she said.

Before I thought about it, I reflexively told her I'd meet her there in 20 minutes, which looking at the traffic on Highway 360 was probably a bit optimistic. About five minutes later, when I was beginning to think I might actually be on time, my phone rang. It was Suzie.

She said she was between patients and had just a few minutes, so I gave her my most succinct description of Roger Hollander's behavior as it had been related to us. The wrinkle, as I saw it was Vivian and her son, Henry. Given his track record back then and more recently, could the presence of a baby or toddler be sufficient to make him alter course?

"Well, I guess it would be odd on its own, but from what Michelle told me about Lisa Jefferson and how the behavior stopped when she became pregnant, perhaps the presence of a child or the 'impurity' of a tattoo somehow exalted or exempted these women in his mind so that he could no longer do what he seems to have done to others," she said.

"So, it sort of makes sense?"

"You know my thoughts on that, Donovan," she said.

"Right. Human beings rarely make sense, but sometimes we can figure why they think the way they do."

"Of course, all of this is speculation since we can't interview Mr. Hollander."

"How's Michelle doing?"

"You know I can't discuss our session with you, but in the most general sense she'll be okay," she said.

I thanked her, hung up and concentrated on the traffic. I had made the turn from Highway 360 onto Highway 183. At the Central Drive exit in Bedford I ducked out and headed to Harwood Road, which at that point was much faster.

* * *

Detective Baker was already waiting for me when I walked in the door at Donut Wheel. She had a small box of donuts and a cup of coffee already going. I bought one of those small cartons of milk and joined her at her table.

"Thanks for calling," she said.

"Thanks for coming out," I said.

I told her about the recent developments in the case and our observations to this point. She listened attentively as she sipped her coffee.

"I'm not really big on repeating 'I'm sorry,' but I am sorry. I went back over my notes this weekend. In fact, I almost did nothing else but think about this case again, and I don't know what to say. Yeah, it was my first big case here in my home town, but we should have seen beyond the bright and shining descriptions everyone was giving us of Hollander," she said.

I shrugged a "What are you gonna do?" kind of shrug. She was sorry and I didn't want to be a jerk. Police work is far from perfect, just like anything else involving human beings.

She asked about Lisa Jefferson, so I told her what happened. She munched on a donut and sipped some more coffee and listened. Toward the end, she put the donut and coffee both down and just listened.

"Geez," she said. "That poor girl. How's your partner?"

"She'll be okay," I said, "eventually."

It still rubbed me the wrong way that we got here in a week and they had the case a year, but I figured that wasn't a year of active investigation time. And I reminded myself that I did have the advantage of looking at the whole picture while they had to put the picture together frame by frame.

She seemed bright enough. Molsby liked her okay, as much as he actually liked anyone. She had the vibe of a good cop, whatever stock you might put in such things. I still didn't want her to know that I had the full case file. I didn't know how tight she was with Molsby, and I didn't want anything blowing back on him.

"So, you said you went back over your notes this weekend. Did anything jump out at you? Anything you didn't think of when we talked about it the first time we met?" I asked.

Most people don't like others second guessing them. Who can blame them? It was pretty obvious that Baker was fine with beating herself up, but she took it that I had started treating her like a witness. Which I more or less had.

"Look, I know you're doing your best to help out Mrs. Hollander, who we both like, and I know your partner had a very bad experience. I know we should have pressed harder beyond the Peter Perfect façade," she said, "but I have been doing this a while and I know how to read my own case notes."

She controlled it, but she was plenty irritated. She stood up, picked up her coffee and box of donuts.

"And like I said, I spent the whole weekend going over them and I didn't find anything new. Call me if you've got something good. Otherwise..." she searched for something not overtly angry to say. "Just call me if you have something real."

She turned, walked out the door, and made a beeline to her car. She never even gave me a donut.

CHAPTER 44

Since I was at Donut Wheel and since I already had the small carton of milk, I bought a glazed donut and sat down to enjoy it. I figured I'd call Molsby later and see if Baker's anger was the temporarily frustrated or permanently alienated type. It's not like it was some big fight or anything, but everyone has an ego. Cops are just like other people. Some are great; some hold grudges. Since Hurst is where I live and work, I try to maintain solid relationships with the law enforcement types. I'd do what I could to smooth it over later.

I finished the donut and went to the car. I started it up and put it in reverse, but put it back in neutral and pulled out my phone and called Kayla Singh. She sounded tired, but glad to hear from me.

"I just wanted to check on you and see how you're doing. I should have called sooner, but this case has taken on an ugly life of its own," I said.

"That's so nice of you, Donovan. I really appreciate it," she said. "Hey, I actually called that therapist you recommended. I talked with her a bit on the phone and I have an appointment tomorrow."

I told her that it was a good move and asked her to give me a call afterward to let me know how it went. She said she would and we said goodbye. It was almost lunchtime, so I decided to stop at Taco Bueno on the way back to the office. I called Michelle to see if she wanted lunch, too. She did, so off I went.

* * *

Back at the office, over the fine dining experience that was a Taco Bueno beef burrito, a taco, hot sauce and a Dr. Pepper, I related the meeting with Detective Baker to Michelle.

"Seems a bit touchy for someone who basically screwed up," Michelle said.

"Well, some people just get defensive before they can really admit they made a mistake. She should have pushed harder, sure, but we have the advantage of looking at the whole picture…"

Michelle finished my sentence: "…while they had to put the picture together piece by piece."

"Oh, I've mentioned that before?" I smiled.

"Is Detective Baker pretty?"

"Not today, but yeah, I guess so."

"You would never let a guy slide like this. It's piss poor police work, Donovan, and you know it. You're good and I'm good and together we're really pretty great, but there's no way we should have gotten this far in a week if they didn't overlook something obvious," she said.

"Here's the thing. Yeah, we have a very realistic theory about the killer's motive, or at least the genesis of his or her motive," I said.

"Her motive," she said.

"With the wounds on Roger Hollander, I just don't think most women, even very angry or very motivated, could have done that."

Michelle took a bite of her taco and shrugged. *Michelle*. Shrugged.

"You just shrugged!"

"No I didn't!" She reflexively denied it, but then you could see it register in her mind. She actually froze for a second before a look of disgust came over her face.

"This is your doing! This is your fault! You and your whole shrug-based communication system!"

I shrugged, naturally.

She almost brought her fist down on her taco, but she stopped herself.

"I think we should take this day off every year from now on," I said and took a sip of my Dr. Pepper. "Can we get back to talking about the case?"

"Yes," Michelle grumbled.

"Let's just say that I agree with you that Detective Baker should have gotten further in this case, but we don't have a suspect any more than she did. We're onto something solid. I'm sure of that. We just need to find out where and to whom it leads. I'm willing to bet that there are more potential suspects than we already know about," I said.

"So, start getting alibis for everyone we know about?"

"Yeah, but first I think we should ask Mrs. Hollander to get us the personnel records for the last few years before Roger was killed. It might be a reach, but for the sake of expediency

I think we can eliminate the ones who had children and the women who were older," I said.

Michelle made notes on all of this.

"And there was a girl Digs mentioned, another one from high school. Her name was Karen Crosby. She probably won't remember me, but I knew her at least in passing at Bell. See if you can find a number for her," I said.

"Okay if we bill Mrs. Hollander for some overtime?"

"Sure. In fact, see if Laura's available. We could use the help," I said.

* * *

A short while later I picked up the phone and called Mrs. Hollander. I told her that we were just working a theory, but that it would really help if we could send Donna Mahaffey at their headquarters a request for personnel files and have it dealt with in an expeditious fashion. She asked if there was any further news on the case. I told her that there was nothing definitive but if there were I would call right away. I informed her I'd met with the police several times as well, and we were continuing to review their investigation while conducting our own new one. She might have been realistic about her chances when she came to us, but I couldn't blame her for still being hopeful. She just wanted the case resolved. If things played out the way I thought they would, she would have her closure, but she'd also have a whole new set of things she would wish she never knew.

After waiting a few minutes, I called Donna Mahaffey's office at Hollander's HQ. She seemed happy to hear from me, the way a quarterback is happy to be hit from the blindside by a safety coming in at full speed. But she took the request and promised she would email the files to Michelle within the next two hours. I thanked her for being so helpful, which I knew was entirely because of Mrs. Hollander.

When I was getting ready to leave, my cell phone rang. It was Digs.

"Hey!" I said.

"Hey, yourself," she said. "Do you still want to get together tonight?"

"Yes. That would be safe to say."

"You're not by yourself, are you?"

"Nope."

"Then I shouldn't tell you what I'm wearing?" she whispered.

"No, not really."

"Is later okay? I just found out I have to go to up to Bell tonight. Apparently Rhonda is in a play and her mom just decided to inform me this afternoon while I was at work. I know you're all crazy for me and all that, but you'll notice that I'm not dragging you to see my niece's high school play," she said.

"And later you'll notice how much I appreciate that," I said. "I actually have a case file to go through, so just call me when you're home."

She said she would.

"Okay. I'll see you then. Love you. Bye," I said and hung up. I turned around because I felt Michelle staring at me, which she was.

"You've gone off the deep end, haven't you?" Michelle

asked.

"Probably," I said. I couldn't even shrug. "Why do you ask?"

"Because you just said you loved her."

"No I didn't," I said reflexively. And then I thought about it. "Oh, crap. Did I just ruin everything?"

"Maybe she didn't hear it. It was very casual," Michelle said.

Panic had almost fully set in when the office phone startled me, as if on purpose.

"Donovan Bay Investigations," I answered, desperate for a distraction.

"I love you, too," Digs said, and then hung up. I couldn't stop grinning until finally I started laughing out loud.

CHAPTER 45

As I was driving home from the office, I thought I spotted the silver Chevy pick-up again, but I lost it in a sea of silver pick-ups. In Manhattan or San Francisco, you might stand out driving a silver pick-up. In the Dallas/Fort Worth area, it was just one more way to blend in. The tinted windows made it stand out a bit more, but not enough to really matter. Still, I turned down a couple of side streets and doubled back a bit before going home to make sure I wasn't followed.

Later, after a salad and a glass of iced tea, I sat on the sofa and started back through the case notes that Molsby had provided for me at the outset. I decided to leave the photos alone and concentrate on the other documents. I flipped through them on my tablet.

I had read the crime scene technicians' reports previously, but I had to admit to myself that I hadn't looked at them in detail until after I had looked at the photos. It was time to read them coolly and unemotionally. For the most part, though, my evaluation of them didn't change.

There had been no sign of forced entry. While there were items broken and displaced by the victim's body when it fell, it was a limited area, suggesting that the killer had been close to him when the attack began. That, of course, made sense since the weapon was a knife or blade of some kind.

As I had noted previously, the immediate area was drenched in the victim's blood. The splatter patterns, which were analyzed in more detail in separate document, were concentrated in the area in which the victim was found, but they actually stretched across the room, giving a measurement to the ferocity of the attack.

Its savage nature suggested that this was a crime of the moment, a crime of passion, not something planned in detail. This would have meant the attacker would have been covered in Roger Hollander's blood, particularly on his or her upper torso, but possibly from head to toe. That also meant that he or she had to have cleaned up before leaving the scene.

The folks at the lab had come up with nothing useful in terms of identifying the killer. The bathroom had been gone over with bleach and other cleaning solutions found under Hollander's sink, but the containers had been wiped clean and the shower curtain had been taken down. If I was the killer and anywhere close to the victim's size, I would have wrapped up the bloodied clothes in the shower curtain and taken some clothes from Hollander's closet or dresser.

I picked up my cell phone and called Mrs. Hollander again. She answered after just two rings. I asked her if the private apartment her son had kept was still intact at their headquarters. She said that of course it had been cleaned up once the police released it, but it was basically as it was then. She asked if I was looking for something specific. I told her

I wasn't, but that I'd like to stop by and see it. She said that I was welcome to do so, even if I wanted to go tonight. They had a training class going on this evening in the building, so there was someone there who could let me in. I told her I'd take her up on that and that I could be there in 20 minutes or so. She said she'd make the arrangements.

I hung up the phone, powered down my tablet, popped it in a messenger bag, grabbed my jacket, my keys and a ball cap, and hit the road.

* * *

On the way to the Hollanders' office, I called Michelle. She was way better than me at visualizing crime scenes after the fact, and I was pretty good myself. I wasn't going to ask her to go with me, but she told me that she'd be ready when I got there. She was still at the office, so she wasn't far from where I was headed. The second time I asked if she was sure she wanted to do it, she hung up on me, so I took it that she thought she was ready. She was waiting outside our office when I pulled up.

* * *

Just a few minutes later we were at Hollander's office and Inez, who had helped me on my previous visit, admitted us to the building. She said that Mrs. Hollander had asked her to give me the key and stick around as long as we needed anything. She also said that she would be there as long as the training class was going on, so we could take our time. She handed me the key and pointed us up the stairs and past Donna Mahaffey's office. We went up the stairs, turned to the left, and went down the hall, past the other offices, closets and a couple of rest rooms. At the end of the corridor was a door that was nicer and more residential-looking. I put the key into the lock and it turned easily.

CHAPTER 46

Roger Hollander's office apartment had been fully cleaned up and repaired, but it looked very much as if it had been restored to how it looked before the crime. Michelle said as much before we got 10 feet inside the door.

She had worked for the Ft. Worth Police Department as a videographer and photographer right out of college and still had an uncanny knack of understanding and explaining cause and effect as various theories were tried, played out, accepted or discarded.

I opened my tablet, and called up some of the basic crime scene photos. Clearly new carpet, painting, some replaced items on the book shelves, new sofa, but it actually was almost like looking at the "before" photos if the ones I got from Molsby were the "after" ones.

Mrs. Hollander had told me that no one was using the apartment at this point. She didn't mention that it was her shrine to her son, restored and preserved as if he might come home to it at any time. Grief works on us all in different ways. I tried to put all that out of my head and get back to business.

Michelle and I walked about the place silently for a few

minutes, getting the feel of it. It was actually a nice set-up, considering it was in the back corner of what was basically a warehouse. The entirety of the view was pretty much a parking lot and a high tech self-storage center.

Back in the 1970s, Pipeline Road had been a good business address. In more recent times, though, with the exception of the portion down by Northeast Mall, it was hard to even keep a brand name fast food business going there. Hollander's headquarters had changed that, tearing down old buildings steeped in decades of failure. If the building itself looked like every other prefabricated warehouse on the outside, the activity inside and even the cars just being in the parking lot brought new life to the area.

What a shame it came from rotten excuse for a human being like Roger Hollander, I thought.

"Okay, let's talk about the feel of the place for a minute before we look at what went down," Michelle said. "In purely business terms, for such a determined and hard worker like Hollander was reputed to be, this place makes a ton of sense. Work late, go up to your nice apartment, grab a shower, get some sleep, hit it again as soon you're ready. But it also makes a lot of sense from the angle of a predator looking to abuse women while minimizing the chance of interruption."

"Because he knew the schedules here, knew when people would be working late and when they wouldn't, could come and go after hours, and most importantly answer to no one," I said.

"Did you see the security camera when we came in?"

"Sure," I said. "New addition?"

"You should check with Baker, but there's nothing about it in the report. And as much as I think she did a half-assed job on this case, you know she didn't miss something like that. We can ask your pal Inez on the way out, too," she said.

"Okay, back to possible scenarios here," I said.

"The way I see it, every way I've tried to work it out in my head or on paper, he either brings someone back here or allows them in once he's already here. He pours some wine, gets out that yearbook you spotted. I'd love to know what motivated his trip down memory lane. The person is right there next to him," she said.

We acted it out several different ways, but it always came back to those basics. If the attacker had a running start at him or if their battle was drawn out prior to him being stabbed, there would have been more incidental damage. We looked at the photos together again and there just wasn't anything to support that interpretation.

The autopsy indicated that there were defensive wounds, but not in keeping the severity of attack. Possible interpretation: the attack came from close up and it came unexpectedly. If that was the case, the attacker had to have been close to him. If it was a man, it almost certainly had to have been someone he knew well.

"He's a predator. He's not going to let a man he perceives as a threat get that close to him without being in a position to defend himself," Michelle said.

"But, as much as I like that theory, say it's a friend or an employee he's known a long time, and that man has found out that Hollander's taken an unhealthy interest in his daughter or younger sister…"

"Possible, but I just don't see it. It could always be that I'm too in love with our theory, but let's think about this in terms of women. We know that he preyed on women he believed he could dominate emotionally as well as physically," she said.

"So, what, he chose incorrectly and the young woman played it cool until she was close and then just pounced?"

"Maybe. I don't know. But I keep seeing this as someone he did this to for a while. Maybe someone who lived through it and saved all the anger up until she had the opportunity to do something about it? I don't know," she said. "I just don't know."

We agreed that it was a least a theory worth pursuing, and we had a list of possible suspects going back years. We turned out the lights and locked up the apartment, went downstairs, gave the key back to Inez, and thanked her. Michelle confirmed with her that the video security camera was a recent instillation, put up as soon as the police had released the crime scene. I would still check with Baker, but that seemed like a dead end.

As we walked across the parking lot to my car, I looked down at my shoes, put my hands in my pockets and tried to walk as nonchalantly as possible.

"What's with you?" Michelle asked.

"Don't look. Just get in the car. That silver pick-up that's been following me is across the lot," I said.

CHAPTER 47

As we got into the car, I glanced at the rearview mirror. The truck was sitting across the lot, lights out. With the ambient sounds from Pipeline Road and Precinct Line Road, it was difficult to tell for certain, but I was pretty sure the truck's engine was running.

"Buckle up," I said to Michelle.

I turned the key and gave it a little extra gas and it started right up with an authoritative roar which then became a solid, purr. Not for the first time, I silently blessed Lido Anthony Iacocca and my mechanics, and I pulled on the headlights.

"Subtle," Michelle said.

"I don't want to lose this idiot," I said as I started to back out of the space. I turned the car and headed toward the Precinct Line Road exit from the lot. I turned left onto Precinct Line and moved slow enough that if he had the slightest inclination to follow me it would be easy.

And he or she did.

"Did you bring your gun?" I asked Michelle.

She looked at me like I was an idiot. She had voted herself Ms. Conceal & Carry for eight years running, much the same way that I had voted myself as a World Class Private Investigator.

"I'm going to go down some of the side streets, not too many turns, but enough that you should be able to call Molsby without whoever this goon is seeing you. I'm going to try to lead him down some side streets toward Barbara Ann Drive and then down onto Hurstview Drive heading up toward Bedford-Euless Road," I said, making a slow turn onto Edgehill Drive. It's a short residential street and no one was out, so I gave it more gas and put a little more room between us. I left the spacing close enough that the driver following us would have seen our brake lights and the turn signal as I turned right onto Forest Oaks Lane.

Michelle quickly called Molsby. We could have called 911, but that risked getting someone on the evening shift who I didn't know. She gave him the info quickly and hung up right away. He'd call it in.

We turned left onto Cheryl Avenue as I saw the headlights behind us turn right onto Forest Oaks Lane. I expected our pursuer to pick up speed here and I wasn't disappointed. By the time we transitioned from Cheryl Avenue onto Barbara Ann Drive, the headlights were closing on us quickly. Too quickly.

The silver Chevy pick-up was almost right on top of us and was headed straight for the back end of my Mustang at what the esteemed Daniel Simpson Day would call "Ramming speed!" On the other hand, the day that tub can catch my car is the day I get a SmartCar. I romped on the accelerator and we flew down Barbara Ann. As the intersection with Hurstview approached, I hoped there was no traffic. It wasn't an obstructed intersection, but this was suburbia. The sightlines weren't like on highway.

"Hold on," I said to Michelle.

I slammed on the brakes, cut the wheel hard to the left and we spun 180 degrees. We came to a stop straight at the oncoming silver Chevy pick-up, which was still closing rapidly. Michelle was out the door with her gun drawn quicker than I was, but we were both ready as it skidded to a stop.

I could hear a police siren, but I couldn't tell from what direction it was coming. The truck just sat there, idling. I nodded to Michelle to cover me and I began walking toward it. In the cab I could just make out a figure that looked like a man. He was either pounding out his frustration on the steering wheel or was keeping rhythm with a drum solo on the radio.

"Turn off the vehicle and step out, hands first," I said loudly in my most cop-like voice. The engine turned off, but the vehicle just sat quietly. For a moment, nothing moved. The siren grew closer, but I still couldn't tell from which direction.

The truck's door opened and a pair of hands came out first, followed by the rest of Larry Green, the store manager for Hollander's Northeast Mall store. The guy I didn't like the first time I met him.

It pissed me off because I knew he didn't do it. What the hell was his problem?

"Michelle, this is Larry Green. Until now he worked for Hollander over at the mall. Managed their store there," I said. "So, I guess you know it's all over, right, Larry?

"I didn't do nothin' wrong," he said. He started to lower

his hands.

"Even your grammar is wrong, Larry. And turn around and put your hands on the truck."

Now everyone could hear the sirens and it was clear they weren't just coming from one direction.

"Why'd you do it?" I said. I had no idea what "it" was, but the cops would be here soon enough and the chances of us getting him to talk were small enough already. What the heck, right?

"It seemed like easy money at first, but then they said if I stopped they'd kill me."

"Well, that makes sense now," I said. I looked at Michelle and shrugged. She didn't even glare back. She just motioned for me to keep going.

"The one thing I don't know is who are 'they,' these people that are going to kill you."

"The TK 88-19s in Fort Worth," he said, his head slumping.

Michelle looked at me with a "What the hell did we just stumble into?" face. I had no more idea than she did. The TK 88-19s were heavy duty gangbangers with ties to serious drug cartels. I couldn't remember the specifics, but I think they were from Honduras. The sirens were getting closer. One or two more questions.

"Listen, I can certainly see why you'd be afraid, and when the time comes you really need to level with the District Attorney about all this. It could help your situation if you do," I said as reassuringly as possible. "How many did they get you for?"

"It was never the same number of sim cards. Just however many they needed to keep their burner phones changing on a regular basis," he said. The sirens grew louder still. His head hung lower.

"So why come after me, after us? Why not just run?"

"And go where?" he said. I had no answer. Three patrol units pulled up. They killed their sirens, but we were bathed in red and blue and white lights. Michelle had her gun back in her purse before they pulled up.

"Are you Bay?" one of the officers asked.

"Yes, I am, officer," I said.

"Molsby sent us. What's the story?"

I filled them in on the basics. They handcuffed Larry Green and put him in the back of one the squad cars. One of the officers moved the truck from the center of the road and parked it along the curb.

Michelle called Molsby and made sure he knew what the details were now that it was over. He had a soft spot for her because of her detail-oriented nature.

I promised to come in early the next morning and give them as much background as I could and answer any questions about the case that we hadn't known anything about until we broke it. When we were finished, Michelle wanted to go through the drive-through at Jack in the Box, which was just up the road at this point. We did so and then I dropped her back at the office.

"You sure do know how to show a girl a good time," she said as she got out of the car. "See you tomorrow."

I started to back out of the space, but then she started

waving and came running over. I stopped. She flashed me her index finger to wait a moment. She dug in her purse and came up with a piece of paper. She came around to my side and I rolled down the window. "I would have remembered this tomorrow, but Karen Crosby, the one you asked me to find from back at L.D. Bell. She called back. Here's her number," she said and handed me the paper.

I thanked her, rolled up the window, and headed toward home.

CHAPTER 48

TUESDAY

As I pulled away from the office, Michelle was getting in her car. I glanced at my watch and was surprised to see it was 12:30 a.m. I was still wired from the night's activities and hadn't noticed time until now. I wondered why Digs hadn't called. Then I saw there were several texts from her starting at 9 p.m.

She had arrived home and still wanted me to come over. She was getting tired and hoped I was okay. If I had fallen asleep with case files, I was going to be very disappointed to have missed what she was wearing. And finally, she was going to sleep, but she had left a spare key in a flowerpot by the front door. That text included her alarm code.

I figured since she was asleep I should just head home, get a shower and go to bed. I could catch up with her in the morning. My shower was better, after all, I told myself. So I headed straight to her place. I let myself in with the key from the flowerpot. I'd have to tell her how precisely unsafe that was, but not now. I deactivated the alarm and made my way to her bedroom.

She was asleep with the covers bunched up all around

her. I kissed her on the forehead and she just kept breathing rhythmically. I took off my jacket, shirt and pants, draped them over a chair, and headed for the bathroom. I stopped and grabbed my phone from my pants pocket. I closed the door and turned on the light. There was a note there telling me to wake her up when I got there, and she had left out towels and a robe if I wanted to take a shower. It made me smile.

When I got out of the shower, I dried off and put on the robe. It was some kind of bulky terrycloth, but it was oddly comfortable. I clicked off the light and opened the door to the bedroom. The lights were still out and Digs was still sleeping soundly.

I slipped under the covers and she didn't even stir. Once I pulled the covers over me, I put my hands between the pillow and my head and looked at the ceiling. I was exhausted, but my mind was racing. Life would have been so much better if Larry Green turned out to be the killer, but he was an idiot, not a murderer. And of course it would have blown my theory apart if it turned out to be him. I closed my eyes and concentrated on trying not to concentrate.

* * *

"Donovan," Digs said quietly, a whisper.

A moment or an hour or a day or a week later, she said it again, louder.

I managed to force one of my eyes to open. She was standing beside the bed. I couldn't quite focus. The lights were still off, but I spied the clock radio on the bedside table. I'd been asleep for maybe two hours. I motioned for her to wait a minute, rubbed my eyes, and sat up, then reached over and turned on the light.

"You were supposed to wake me up when you got here," she said with a smile.

Suddenly, I was pretty much awake.

* * *

Later, we sat mostly under the covers, her leaning against me, head on my shoulder, her hand rubbing my chest slowly, propped up by pillows, not really watching the old show she had found on Netflix. The only light in the room came from the TV.

"Listen, I don't want this to sound awkward or weird or anything…" she said.

"Which it doesn't at all with a preamble like that," I said.

She swatted me gently with the hand that had been rubbing before.

"I said 'listen' first, didn't I?"

"Point taken."

"I don't mean anything more than I'm actually saying, okay? But I just wanted you to know that if you want to, it would be okay if you wanted to leave some clothes over here," she said. She resumed rubbing my chest.

The angle would have made it hard for her to see my face, so it made sense that after a few moments she took my silence as me being uncomfortable. She couldn't see that I was smiling.

"Maybe it wasn't the right time to – "

I cut her off.

"Shhhh," I said very quietly. "It's fine. I think it's an okay idea."

"Good," she whispered and leaned in closer.

I was quiet, just absorbing everything, enjoying it.

"I'm glad you came over," she whispered.

"Me, too."

"Why are we whispering?" she asked.

I turned and looked her in the eyes.

"Because suddenly every sordid, vile, crappy, horrible thing I'd discovered this past week was put into perspective," I said, "and it just seems right."

CHAPTER 49

The next morning I was a little bit late getting to the office. For that matter, Digs was also a little bit late, too, but I'm sure it was a coincidence. Michelle and Laura were using our two white boards – known affectionately as "the white board" and "the emergency extra white board" – to make a grid of the Hollanders' employees we should consider talking with and those who, at least for our purposes right now, we could eliminate. They clearly had been at it a while.

"What happened to coming in a bit late?" I asked as I hung my jacket over the back of my chair and dropped my ball cap on my desk.

"Don't look at me," Laura said as she shuffled a couple of files and apparently found what she was looking for. "I just told her to call me when she got here."

"Believe it or not, I slept fine, but I woke up early and getting at this was really on my mind," Michelle said. "At least you got to sleep in a bit."

"Yep," I said and intently studied what they were doing. "How long a period before the murder are we searching?"

"Five years. Completely arbitrary guess on my part, but

we had to start somewhere. Laura already did a spreadsheet of this in the computer, but we're taking a measure twice, cut once approach," Michelle said. "Have you been in to talk to the detectives about Larry Green yet?"

"Nope. Wanted to see how things were going here."

"They called and asked me to come over at 2 p.m.," she said.

"Sounds like Ring Culper's on the case," I said. I sat down and leaned back in my chair. "He was the one that called, right?"

"Ring does *not* have a crush on me," Donovan.

"Okay," I said.

She stopped looking through the file and used her laser vision on me. It didn't work.

"I'm just saying, Michelle, that it's a little odd that first thing in the morning the Hurst Police Department makes an appointment with you an hour before the morning shift ends, so Ring might be free to go get a beverage or an early dinner with you."

She started sorting through papers again.

Officially ignoring me.

The phone rang. She made no move to get it.

"I'll get this one," I said to Laura, who just looked back down at her laptop, then reached over and made another "X" on the first white board.

"Donovan Bay Investigations," I said.

"Molsby," said Molsby.

"Morning," I said since we were going with the one-word motif.

"Interview?"

"Now?"

"Yes."

"Okay."

He hung up, so I hung up. Michelle was looking at me. "He started it," I said.

"You are a very strange man, Donovan," she said.

* * *

Hurst Police Department headquarters was its usual quiet hive of activity when I got there just a few minutes later. I only got as far saying "Donovan Bay here to see – " before the officer at the front desk politely cut me off. She was not the one who had been there on my last visit, but they could have been related.

"Detective Culper, the Tarrant County District Attorney, Special Agent in Charge Carson, a man from the DEA, and the Assistant U.S. Attorney are just finishing up a phone conference, Mr. Bay. They asked for you to please have a seat. It shouldn't be more than five or 10 minutes," she said with a soft, beautiful blend of southern and Texas twangs.

Less than three minutes later, Molsby appeared in the doorway and waved me back. Like his phone conversations, it was a single gesture. Fail to obey at your own peril. Indicating I should keep quiet, he ushered me into a room with the DA, who I knew, and three men I didn't know but who I took to be FBI, DEA and the Asst. U.S. Attorney for the region. The DA was thanking whomever they were talking to on the speaker phone. The call ended.

Molbsy nodded to the DA.

"Gentlemen, this is Mr. Bay, the private investigator based here in Hurst who gave our case such a big boost last night," the DA said. I could tell by the way he said "based here in Hurst" that I had somehow put some sort of feather in his cap. Hoorah for the home team and all that.

The DA introduced me to Special Agent in Charge Carson, FBI, Agent David Meddings, DEA, and Assistant U.S. Attorney Crenshaw Hamper, all of whom along with Culper greeted me as if I'd hit a homerun to win the game. If you thought about it, it was more like I got hit by a pitch to drive in the winning run, but a win was a win even if I didn't particularly like these guys thinking I'd done something great instead of just something good.

"Mr. Bay, District Attorney Abernathy, Detective Culper and Sgt. Molsby have vouched for you and requested you be read-in on this one. And given your assistance, I certainly had no objections," Hamper said. "The TK 88-19s street gang in Ft. Worth have been a major problem for local law enforcement and those of us at the Federal level. Larry Green has been illegally supplying them with sim cards and providing other assistance so they can use their burner phones with even less chance that we could ever catch them. Now he's going to continue feeding sim cards to the gang, only they'll be ones we're supplying. And we expect that to make Ft. Worth and the rest of Tarrant County safer for everyone."

He reached out his hand to shake mine. I hesitated but didn't leave him hanging. The others in the room applauded. This was a little too much. Molsby sensed my discomfort and smiled, the ruthless bastard.

"I'm really glad what I uncovered helped, but I was just
– "

The DA cut me off.

"Gentlemen, I know you need to get back to Fort Worth,"
he said. There was more quick small talk, shaking of hands
and even a pat on the back, and then they were gone and it was
just the DA, Molsby and me.

"No more high-speed chases through residential
neighborhoods in Hurst, Donovan," the DA said.

"Yes, sir," I said.

"Good. It was a remarkably timely arrest. They were
going to lose some Federal funding for their task force if they
didn't get some traction soon. I don't mind those guys owing
us in Hurst a little. Do you?"

"No, sir," I said.

"I didn't think you would. Detective Culper, he's all
yours. I know you have a few questions for him."

"Can't wait," I said.

* * *

I finished talking with Detective Duwayne Culper, better
known as "Ring," after about an hour and 15 minutes and
figured it was time for lunch. When I got in the car, I decided to
try Karen Crosby's number before I hit the road. She answered
after four rings.

To my surprise – okay, to my complete and utter shock
– she not only remembered me, she remembered that I wrote
a history paper for her that bailed her out and brought up her
grade enough that she could stay on the cheerleading squad.
She sounded very upbeat, but said I caught her as she was

headed out the door.

"It's really weird that you called now. I haven't been home to Texas in almost three years, but I'm headed there tonight. My brother's getting married and there's a big engagement party at my parents' place," she said. "Maybe we could get together for lunch or something?"

I asked her to give me a call when she got settled here and said that we could work out a time to meet. She said she would. I didn't expect her information to lead to anything, but the way the day had gone thus far, I really couldn't rule it out.

And no matter how my disposition had improved since the night before, we still needed a break.

CHAPTER 50

Michelle and Laura didn't want Taco Bueno for lunch – *Who can understand the workings of the criminal mind?* – so I offered to pick them up something else. They couldn't decide what they wanted, so I told them I'd call back after I finished eating.

The work and social portions of my life seemed like polar opposites when I came to work that morning, but the Larry Green bust could actually turn out to be great for business. It wasn't as if the DEA or the FBI or the Assistant U.S. Attorney were about to hire us or even send clients our way, but in a business in which information is king, you can never have too many official contacts. It definitely wouldn't hurt our standing with the Tarrant County District Attorney either.

And things with Digs were significantly better than what teenage me always dreamed they would be. I wished I could tell teenage me that he was right, tell him to open his eyes and see that Nancy Esplen was crazy about him, tell angry late-20s me that I couldn't fix what was wrong with Janice Baldwin by hanging in there, and tell wounded me just a few years back that things with Digs would heal, and eventually get better, it would get a lot better.

My usual beef burrito, Taco and Dr. Pepper were perfect, so I took my time eating and enjoyed them. When I finished, I called Michelle. She and Laura wanted salads and had called in their orders. All I had to was stop by and pick them up and then head back to the office.

* * *

The rest of the afternoon was spent going through the files that Donna Mahaffey had sent over at Mrs. Hollander's direction. Michelle and Laura had done an excellent job, both logically and with the guesswork. Like Michelle had said earlier, we had to pick an arbitrary cut-off point and five years seemed fine.

They had eliminated women with children. They had eliminated women over 30. Given that he had attacked white women, Hispanic women, an ethnically Indian woman, we agreed that we would not eliminate any of the possibilities based solely on race or ethnicity.

That's right, Mrs. Hollander. Your son was a vile character, a destroyer of lives, but you can be proud he wasn't a racist.

We gave it some debate, but in the end we eliminated married women, even the younger ones, only because we didn't have anything thus far that would lead us to believe that he had attacked married women.

In the end this left us with a manageable group. Sorting through them and researching them all wouldn't automatically find us a suspect, but we were all still in agreement that this was something we had to do. It would take a while to research and locate them if they were still in the area, but it was doable.

Laura had to go back to work at the library the following day, but she said she could help out over the weekend or even at night.

There would be a lot more hard work ahead, but it felt like we were getting somewhere. Michelle started organizing the printouts and Laura did likewise.

"What happened with Karen Crosby? Did you get a hold of her?" Michelle asked as she organized the place. She couldn't leave it messy even though she knew we would come in tomorrow and mess it up all over again.

"Oh, yeah. She called back. She's coming into town tomorrow for a family thing and we'll get together at some point. It may be another dead end, but I've still got to follow-up on it," I said.

"She was pretty cute back in the day," Laura said.

I nodded but not too emphatically. Or so I thought.

"Was there a cute girl you didn't have a thing for back then?" Laura asked.

"What?" I asked, innocent and all that.

"Really? Were you just like one big gland in high school?" Michelle asked, not missing a beat in her clean-up.

"Where's the yearbook I brought you?" I asked.

She didn't look. She just pointed sharply with her left hand to a small table on the other side of her desk. And there it was. I walked over to it, opened it up, and flipped through until I found the page with Karen Crosby's photo on it. One look at it and I certainly wasn't going to question my judgment back then. I showed the picture to Michelle.

"Well, she was pretty awesome looking," she said. "And

you were pretty much, you know, not."

"Hey, he was cute," Laura said.

"Spare me the teen drama. I feel like I'm watching *90210* back in the day," Michelle said.

I looked at Karen's picture a moment and was going to flip to Laura's to show Michelle when I saw it. On the next page, one page over from Karen. It had been freakin' in front of me all along. My gut had told me something was wrong and I ignored it.

There was a picture of a girl I had passed in the school's hallways many times, but I never put her face together with the name of one of the popular people I always heard about back then. Her individual photo was much better than the semi-obscured one of her in the French club at L.D. Bell.

Ginger Davis. Only her name was Ginger Baker now. Detective Ginger Baker.

CHAPTER 51

I loved Nick Molsby like a big, demented, imposing, passive-aggressive, monosyllabic, crime-fighting uncle, and my first instinct was to go to running to him like a four-year-old with a skinned knee and tell him everything we had found, everything I suspected, everything I felt about this case. What saved me from the results of doing so was the thought of him saying, "Okay, that's good. What can you *prove*?"

The answer, of course, was "Nothing. Yet." So I showed Michelle and Laura my discovery. They both immediately pointed out that Ginger Baker going to Bell didn't mean she had somehow known the much older Roger Hollander and then killed him many years later. I countered with my belief that her presence in the French club photo and the book being opened to that page at the crime scene was too much to ignore.

Of course the police investigation didn't find any of the background stuff that we found. She didn't want it to!

This revelation was not going to bring the case to a close that night. I needed to think it over calmly and plot our moves very carefully, do nothing impulsively. And as much as things were screaming and waving their hands that they were falling into place, I put the brakes on.

I told Michelle and Laura they were right, and we couldn't give up on the process just because of the presence of Ginger in that photo. We'd have to review it less emotionally tomorrow. I don't know whether they believed me or not, but we left it at that.

"What are you going to do?" Laura asked.

"I have no idea," I said.

* * *

This was no mere stress that I could shake by driving around listening to music. This required a trip to the gym. I hadn't been since the day before we started this case, so I felt rusty. That disappeared after about 20 minutes on the treadmill. I've never had the best discipline about the gym, but one thing I know for certain is that there are very few times in my life when I'm only doing one thing. The gym is one of them. Once I get going, I simply exist, I just do what I am doing right then at that moment. The next minute, the next five minutes, the next miles. The goal becomes the thing, even if I have to lie to myself that it's just five more minutes. Money, cases, family, relationships, taxes, car problems, they all just fade. Even though we work out for our bodies, it's actually probably the best thing I do for my brain. It's really hard to overestimate the clutter and distraction of our daily lives, how many things we try to multi-task, even people who would swear they didn't multi-task.

I went another 40 minutes before I hit the sit-ups and push-ups, which I had always hated. I had left the office early, so the place wasn't filled up with the usual rush hour crowd. It was almost deserted, so I didn't try to hide the grunting sounds as I hit another set of sit-ups.

Detective Baker wasn't entirely fading, no matter how hard I pushed, but my head was clearing on the subject. She was a cop. She deserved the benefit of the doubt, no matter how it looked, the same thing *any* suspect deserved. The only thing I personally owed her was the chance for her tell me about it face to face.

Before I hit the shower, I called her line at the department. She answered.

"I'm really sorry for how I came across before. I didn't mean to step on your toes, and if there's one person who I know is frustrated about this case, I know it's you," I said.

She grumbled something.

"Can I buy you lunch at Sutherland's tomorrow? I think I have a lead that might really go somewhere."

She was silent for a moment, but then agreed. We agreed to meet there at noon and then hung up. After that I called Tyler.

"What up, dog?" he said instead of "Hello."

"Does talking that way give you more street cred?" I asked.

"Sure it does," he said. "What can I do for you?"

"I need you to take Molsby to Sutherland's at noon tomorrow. It's on me, but don't tell him that. See if you can't make it 10 or 15 minutes before that, but eat slow, lots of chit chat."

"Molsby? Chit chat? Who is this *really*?"

"I'm bringing someone there. We'll get there at noon. I

need back-up without it appearing to be anything more than a coincidence that you're there. And I might need him to be there, but I don't need him to know that. Make sure you get one of those tables too small for four people and that you're in a part of the main dining area with good sightlines to the rest of the room," I said.

"Okay," he said, understanding that I knew he was funny but that this wasn't the time. It occurred to me that now I knew how Michelle felt most of the time. I told him that she could give him some petty cash in the morning if he needed an advance to cover it, only since we hadn't been paid yet on the comic book caper.

"Got it covered, but I'll keep the receipts," he said. After we finished our call, I headed for the shower. It felt good and I couldn't wait to see Digs.

CHAPTER 52

On my way home from the gym, Karen Crosby called me back. She asked if we could meet tomorrow afternoon. She said anytime after 2 p.m. would work best, unless I wanted to meet up later that night. I told her I'd have to pass on doing anything this evening since I had a previous commitment.

"Sounds like I'm just back in town and already being blown off in favor of another woman," she laughed. I remembered liking her laugh in high school. It wasn't a polite chuckle; it was a real laugh.

"Well, something like that," I said.

"I always thought you'd end up with Digs O'Conner or the Laura girl. What was her name?"

"Laura Field."

"That's it! Laura Field. What's she doing these days?"

"She practically runs the Hurst Library. You should see the place since they expanded it. It's amazing," I said.

"And what about Digs?"

"This will probably make you laugh even more, but we just started seeing each other last week," I said. I had no idea why I was telling Karen Crosby this. I hadn't seen her in 20 years and had only rarely thought of her since we graduated. But there I was.

And I was right. She laughed heartily. "You're kidding!"

I assured her I wasn't, and she laughed some more. We made plans to meet at 2:30 p.m. the following day and then hung up. I had no idea what Karen looked like these days, but as we established previously she was pretty awesome back when. I knew it was some mild vanity, but I didn't mind telling one hot girl from high school that I was seeing another hot girl from high school.

A couple minutes later I pulled up out front of my place. I wasn't going to be long. I was just checking my mail and messages and grabbing a change of clothes and heading toward Digs' place. She had told me to keep the key from the flower pot for the time being, a comment that made me decide to forget for right now about telling her the security risks of common hiding places for keys.

* * *

Since I got to Digs' house before she did, I decided to make enchiladas and a big salad for our dinner. I got her text just as I pulled into her driveway. She was tied up in a meeting. She mentioned being bored out of her skull, which I presumed she meant figuratively. That actually gave me more than enough time to do a really good job with the dinner and have it ready even before she walked in the door. I don't know if enchiladas and salads count as candlelight dinner material, but I threw caution to the wind and went with the idea.

* * *

When she came through the front door carrying her laptop

bag and her purse, she actually seemed a little blown away by my efforts. That was a cool thing to experience.

She got cleaned up and we sat down at her dining room table and enjoyed the meal. She told me about her day and I told her about anything except the case. I wasn't going to pollute the best thing in my life anymore than I had to with that case. I did tell her about Larry Green and how that had worked out, but even then I left out the mention of Hollander's company. If she asked, I wasn't about to lie, but if she didn't I wasn't going to mention it.

After dinner, she went to get changed out of her work clothes and to take a quick shower since I insisted on clearing the table and doing the dishes, which to that point in life had been entirely unlike me.

"But I don't do windows," I said.

She laughed and said she'd be right back.

While she was in the shower, the phone rang. I yelled into the bathroom that the caller ID said it was her sister. She yelled back for me to go ahead and answer it.

"Hey, Juliet," I said. Everyone called her "Jules." Everyone except me, as far as I knew.

"Donovan?" It was a clear connection.

"Yep. How are you?"

"It's good to hear your voice. Where's Digs?"

"She's in the shower. We just had dinner. What's going on? Where are you?"

"I'm in Hawaii. Our transport had a mechanical and I'm stuck here for three days at taxpayer expense. It's horrible," she said. "Hey, so by dinner you mean you splurged for Taco

Bueno, right?"

"Funny. I cooked your sister dinner and even did the dishes."

"You always were her slave."

"More so than ever, it would seem," I said.

"Wait a minute! Is there something actually going on back there?"

"I think you ought to talk to her about that," I said.

"You're kidding! You and my sister? When did this happen? I didn't even think you guys were talking that much these days," she said. She sounded genuinely pleased, which was good. If she wasn't pleased, she was always an excellent shot.

"Yeah, well, like I said, I think you ought to talk with her. Are you going to be home anytime soon?"

"Maybe in a few months. Nothing definite. It's been almost three years. Can you believe that?"

I told her that I couldn't believe it had been that long, and that it had been even longer since I saw her. I asked if she wanted me to have Digs call her or wanted me to take a message. She said she was headed out with some friends to hit the beach and that she'd call her sister tomorrow.

We talked for a couple more minutes and then hung up. I liked them both and was glad Jules seemed to be happy about her sister and me.

* * *

When Digs came back into the living room, she was wearing sweatpants and a T-shirt with an image of Superman on it, but the logo over it read "Garfield." I asked her about it and she informed me that it was "ironic." Rather than quibble over semantics, I chose to be mystified by how this girl could be so cute and not just explode.

She squeezed tight up against me as we watched a rerun of *Psych*. We sat watching the show in silence for a few more minutes before she spoke again.

"Are you trying to not let this go too fast? Because I'm trying to not let this go too fast," she said. "I know we're just a few days in to this version of you and me, but we're also a million years into the overall version of you and me."

"Yeah," I nodded. "I'm trying to not desperately want this to work out because as perfect as it feels right now, I don't want to take anything for granted. We're still people. We'll still make mistakes. But I feel like maybe we've both made enough mistakes in the past that maybe we'll do this right or mostly right."

"When did you get so smart?"

"I'm not smart. I'm observant. I work a lot of divorce cases for smart people. It's made me a realist. Or something. I don't know," I said.

"I know you're right and we're new at this part of our relationship," she said, "and I really hope you won't think that we're already falling into a rut..."

"What do you mean?" I asked.

"I have some more sexy, highly impractical, frequently uncomfortable lingerie of questionable functionality that I'd like you to evaluate," she said. "If you're interested."

I assured her I would be glad to help evaluate it, but only in the interests of science. She said she suspected that might be the case, but didn't want to assume.

"Give me five minutes," she said. And I did.

CHAPTER 53

WEDNESDAY

I made sure that Michelle didn't need anything from me at the office that morning. I stopped by long enough to fill her in on my plan and was pleasantly surprised to be able to take the newly arrived check from Jeff Veytia to the bank. It wasn't a large amount, but it was respectable and the case was closed. Good enough work.

As props for my impending lunchtime discussion, I used our good quality paper and printed out two photographs. The first one was the crime scene photo showing the L.D. Bell yearbook open to the page with the French club photo on it. The second was a good, clean scan of the yearbook photo itself, with young Ginger Davis front and center. I also printed out some bullet points from the case.

Over the years, both in my earlier career in law enforcement and since then as private investigator, I've taken down enough people that the anticipation of doing so didn't make me squirrelly. It absolutely heightened my situational awareness, but it didn't make me fidget or make my stomach do flip-flops. But this was a cop. I didn't really know her, but I liked her from our first meeting. I hoped she would prove me wrong and somehow explain away the slipshod investigation and highly unlikely coincidence about the photo.

There was always a chance I was wrong. In the end, I didn't tell Molsby about this ahead of time. He would have been obligated to report it up the chain of command and I didn't want him to take anymore lumps than he would anyway if I had totally missed the boat with this one.

I wanted to be wrong, but I just didn't think I was.

My cell phone rang. It was Tyler. He confirmed that everything was in motion and that he and Molsby would be there at 11:45 a.m. He was at ESC Key Comics. Wednesday was the day new comic books were released, he said, and it was probably going to become his regular shop because they now offered him an excellent discount.

"You're out buying comics before you go on a case?"

"Gotta keep your priorities straight, man," he said. He was quiet for a moment, then more seriously added, "Routine helps me stay focused. I'll be there and I'll have your back, *whatever* this is."

If I had been him, I would have been irritated about not knowing what was really going on, so I didn't blame him.

* * *

I got to Sutherland's about seven minutes early. I saw Tyler's car and Molsby's cruiser in the lot. I didn't see Baker's, so I sat in the lot for five minutes before I went in. Once inside I waited in the lobby for Baker rather than being seated. She arrived right on time. She was dressed similar to how she was for court the other day, and she looked very nice.

"Hey, thanks for coming," I held out my hand to her. She

shook it.

"Thanks for the invitation," she said.

The hostess took us to our seats. Tyler and Molsby didn't see us immediately, but they were right where I wanted them to be. Our table was also well situated. It put her back to Tyler, but it meant he could see me without attracting her attention doing do. She noticed the notebook I was carrying and set on the table, but didn't say anything about it.

We each ordered one of their lunch specials – she got a cheeseburger and fries and I got soup and salad – and we each got iced tea.

"So, tell me about your possible new lead on the Hollander case," she said.

"Okay. We've already covered a bit of the background of Roger Hollander and his propensity for relationships with much younger, vulnerable women," I said. I told her that his track record stretched from at least his late high school days through the time of his death. I spelled out that the number of women we knew about and a pattern that I believed would probably reflect many whom we had not yet confirmed.

I opened my folder, pulled out a page of bullet point items, and handed it to her. I rattled through it, and then handed her a second sheet, which included the Larry Green bust. I played up my connection to the guys I had met after that arrest because it was great filler material. And it seemed to be working because at the very least I had her attention.

"But I'm getting ahead of myself," I said. "To get you to where I thought I could solve this case, let me take you back to the crime scene itself. In particular, to the one crime scene photo that made sure I couldn't forget this case even if I wanted to – and believe me, I sure have wanted to."

I handed her the printout of the photo showing the scene and yearbook. She looked at it.

"I've seen this, but I don't see what it has to – "

"Detective, if you'll allow me...?"

"Sorry, go ahead."

"I know this will sound crazy to you, because quite frankly it sounds crazy to me, but I took one look at this photo and recognized that book you see sitting open there," I tapped the yearbook in the photo.

"What is it?" she asked. If she was faking, I wouldn't want to play poker with her.

I handed her the printout of the yearbook page. The French club.

"Oh, shit," she said quietly.

CHAPTER 54

I told Detective Baker I had a very similar reaction when I first saw the crime scene photo. "The dumbest luck, really. I recognized it upside down because I worked on that particular page when I was on the yearbook staff. A million years and I couldn't have made this happen this way.

"How could I have missed that?" She seemed stunned and that seemed reasonable.

"Tell me what happened."

"I didn't pay any attention to that book. I saw what it was in the generic sense, a yearbook, but I didn't actually look at it," she said, eyes fixed on the two photos.

"Detective Baker... Ginger, I think you knew Roger Hollander when you were at L.D. Bell High School," I said. She brought her gaze up to mine. She blinked a few times.

"I did," she said. It was almost a whisper.

She was still staring at the photos.

"Given this long list of women against whom he committed horrible acts, I hope you will understand that I have to ask you if he assaulted you when you knew him back then."

That snapped her back to the present. She stared fire at

me, her laser vision bored holes through my head, and her head spun around like in *The Exorcist*. Or she was just really angry. I met her gaze and didn't yield.

She dropped her head, again, and looked at her lap. She didn't say anything. Her body tensed like she was going to get up and run out of the place, but then she relaxed again, like a bit of the air went out of her.

"You don't have to tell me about it, Ginger, but it's going to come out," I said. "Help me understand this."

She was quiet for several minutes. She wiped a tear away from one eye and she exhaled slowly and deliberately, like a smoker who had just finished a smoke break. She drummed her fingers on the table twice.

The waiter chose that moment to arrive with our food. He put our respective orders down in front of us. I nodded to him but didn't say anything. He took the hint and didn't try to be chatty. Baker opened her mouth to talk, but nothing came out.

"Take your time," I said. "We are in no hurry."

I didn't want to make any sudden moves, but I slowly took a sip of my iced tea, set it down, picked up a spoon and tried some of my soup. I didn't particularly think eating was a great move right then, but I wanted to do anything I could to appear normal and non-threatening. That was the only thing I could think of.

Baker kept quiet and kept breathing. Finally, she looked up at me again.

When she started talking, it was the same story I'd heard from the other women. No great twists. No happy surprises. Raped. Abused and humiliated both physically and mentally by a man who at first she thought she was lucky to date. She didn't feel like anything special until he had asked her out. They had gone out four times before it happened. Except for a few of the details, I could have told the story. I wanted to reach out and take her hand, but I just let her talk.

Of course she had been traumatized by all of it, she said. She had wanted to kill herself but didn't want to hurt her parents. She eventually got into therapy her senior year in high school and stuck with it. She had gone off to college, been married, been divorced, and then she had the opportunity to move back to Hurst on her own terms.

Hollander hadn't had the warehouse – or therefore the warehouse apartment – back when she was in high school, so she didn't immediately make the connection from the corporate name and address when she got the call. She was, she said, on the way back from the dentist and on her way to the office when she got the call.

She had just skipped a major piece, but I let her continue.

Baker said that uniformed officers were already on the scene. Nothing had even been roped off yet, but they were able to show her straight up to the body in the second floor apartment. When she saw Roger Hollander there, she knew immediately who he was and formed an idea of what had happened just as quickly.

"Right then, right there, that's when I decided that this one wasn't going to get my 'A' game," she said. "Whoever did this probably went through exactly what I did. I'd have to bust my rear end and close a lot of other cases quickly to gloss over not closing this one, but I couldn't stand the thought of taking someone down for doing what someone should have done 20 years ago."

She was boldly and forthrightly confessing to doing a less than stellar job on the case, but that was it. My stomach had transformed into one tightly wound knot.

"Then I met his mom and she sort of humanized the case for me. I actually did put some effort into it after that, but maybe I'd gone too far down that road. I don't know. I have no idea what I would have done if I had found it was some poor other girl he'd done this to..."

It was a plausible cover, at least to start with, and if she was smart she'd stick with it. Worse yet, I was starting to believe her. But there was still the matter of the yearbook. That didn't wash away so easily, and she certainly would be my candidate for cleaning up so well at the crime scene.

"That all seems pretty understandable to me, Ginger," I said calmly. "I hope you'll understand that I have to ask you about what you were doing the night of the murder."

"What? Oh, yeah, at this point that only makes sense," she said. "I had been to Houston on an overnight. I had just met this guy and we went to a concert. I stayed overnight and flew into Love Field early that morning."

I think I just stared at her.

"I know. Who flies early in the morning to make a dental appointment? But that's how it worked out. I'm sure I've got my itinerary on my laptop still, but I can give you the guy's name and information and you can check with Southwest Airlines, too," she said.

Across the restaurant, Tyler and Molsby were finishing

up. I gave him a slight nod so he would know it was okay to leave. I didn't have any freakin' idea what to say next. Molsby spotted us and saved me the trouble.

He walked over and talked in the Molsby way. Baker looked like she wondered when I was going to say something. Tyler introduced himself since Molsby wasn't going to and since my brain had more or less frozen. After a few minutes, they left.

"Send me the boyfriend's number. I'll check it out and get back to you."

"Then what?" she asked.

I put enough money on the table for the meal and a good tip, stood up and left without answering her.

Damn it.

CHAPTER 55

Although Sutherland's isn't far at all from the Panera Bread location where Karen Crosby and I had agreed to meet at 2:30 p.m., I had absolutely no memory of driving there. None. I found myself in its parking lot, my forearms aching because I was holding the steering wheel so tightly. My foot was on the brake, but I had not put the car in neutral. If anyone had been watching me, I'm sure I looked like either someone about to go postal or some kind of zombie or something. I shifted the gearshift into neutral, engaged the parking brake, and shut off the car.

I felt like I'd had too much Nyquil the previous night, cobwebs in my brain, like life and I were moving at different speeds. I tried to shake it off. I rolled down the windows a bit. It was little cooler today and that helped a bit. After I looked around and didn't see anybody paying attention to me, I called Michelle and told her that I'd have to confirm Detective Baker's alibi, but in the meantime she should keep working on the list she and Laura had been assembling.

And I knew Baker's alibi was going to check out. Why *shouldn't* one more thing about this case be screwed up? More work ahead. Okay. More horrible stories ahead. Well, that was going to go with the territory, wasn't it? I remember thinking that private investigation would be a great career field, one that I would like. I screamed in frustration before I remembered the windows were down. I was grateful that we were past the lunch rush and that there was no one outside in the immediate area at the moment.

Although I was 20 minutes early, I went inside and ordered a green tea. I got it and sat down at a table by the window. I zoned out again for a few minutes, but not to the same extent as before. I was alert enough when I saw her entering the building.

Karen was a grown-up version of the Karen I knew in high school. She was every bit as pretty, but she wore it more comfortably, like she wasn't trying to prove anything to anyone. I watched her for just a moment and then waved to catch her attention and stood up to greet her.

She gave me a big hug and told me it was great to see me. At the counter, she ordered a coffee and I got another green tea, and then we sat down. I almost laughed when she told me I looked great.

When she asked what I did for a living, I told her that I had gone to school for criminology and history, had been a cop and was now a private investigator. She said she always had thought I'd be something creative, but then said, "I bet you have to be creative in your job, too."

She was the pastor of a small, nondenominational church – 26 people at last count – in East St. Louis, Illinois. Right across the river from St. Louis, East St. Louis has long been the poster child of American cities you wouldn't want to visit. It was famous for looking bombed out. Once a town of about 90,000, its scarred and abandoned buildings now were home to about 32,000. Things were turning around there, she said, but there were people in that area who had been poor for generations.

"How did you end up in East St. Louis? I can't say that's a direction I saw your life heading back in high school," I said.

"That's a long story, but I can give you the short version," she said. She took a sip of her coffee and nodded at it. "Not bad. You want to hear the story?"

I told her I did.

"After high school, my life fell apart. My parents were getting a divorce and they didn't know what had happened to me. I went off to college, got involved with men and drugs – and I mean a lot of men and a lot of drugs – and alcohol and about as much destructive behavior as I could. Somehow I managed to keep okay grades for about two years, and then the bottom fell out. I lost my scholarship, got kicked out of school, and then got sentenced to six months for transporting drugs for this guy and 90 days for prostitution. But I managed to lie my way into a program for first time offenders that ended up saving my life," she said.

She looked at me and laughed.

"Donovan, it's okay to be a little freaked out. You don't have to hide it. It's not like I had a career in real estate and volunteered in the local literacy program. I was on the honor roll and ended up turning tricks for drug money! When I talk about it now, it's like it happened to somebody else," she said.

"Geez, Karen…" was all I could manage.

She patted my hand as if I was a little kid.

"But wait, there's more," she said and laughed again. "Listen to this: I got clean, got a job, got back in school, found a man, fell in love, got married, and was about to graduate when I got breast cancer. My husband left me, took my savings – it wasn't a lot, but it was all I had – and then I lost my job."

This was one of those rare moments when I didn't know what to say and managed to keep my mouth shut anyway.

"But I survived breast cancer and finally ended up with the one job I apparently had been training for my entire adult life. Even if I was so inclined, there's just about nobody I would have the right to look down on. Anyway, it's hard to look down when you're so busy looking up," she motioned up, but I deduced that she didn't mean the drop ceiling.

"So, not that life on the streets made me a cynic, but I'm betting that you didn't just contact me out of the blue for no reason."

"When your life started falling apart, was it because of Roger Hollander?" If she was going to be that blunt about her own life, I owed her the same level of respect.

She took another sip of her coffee.

"Yes," she said and nodded. She started to explain, but I stopped her and rattled off the basics of the story, the elements common to all of the different women we had spoken with. Without naming them, I told her about Sandy Schulz, Ginger Davis, Lisa Jefferson, and Kayla Singh.

"So many," she said, shaking her head slowly. "I can't imagine how troubled he was and how through him so much more pain was brought into the world. How horrible. While I was trapped in the situation that thought never occurred to me. I even tried to kill myself when we were still at Bell."

I thought we were done with the surprises.

"It was my senior year, so you had already graduated. I cut my wrists in the rest room after school. Digs found me, called 911, and stayed with me until they got there. She even went to the hospital with me. I told her everything and as far I know she's never told a soul. I always thought she was very cool for that," she said.

I agreed. Keeping a confidence was a rare thing, and yeah, Digs was pretty cool.

We sat and talked more about her life. It definitely wasn't what she had expected when I was doing her homework. She said that Jesus ate with the sinners and tax collectors, so she'd be in good company.

"Except for the tax collectors," she laughed.

CHAPTER 56

After Karen went off to join her family for her brother's wedding party, I sat in my car for a few minutes. What she had told me certainly put the rest of the day into perspective. Sure, I had every right to be mad at Detective Baker for phoning it in and probably even hindering the investigation. But I had no doubt what Roger Hollander had done to her and that it had irrevocably altered her life, no matter how it had turned out. As much as we needed the income, I decided that we were going to drop the case.

I called Michelle and told her what I wanted to do. She said she was fine with it and could have a final bill with all of our expenses, including Laura's help, done up by the following day. She asked if I wanted her to talk me out of it, which she probably could have done. I asked her if she thought it was the right decision. After all, she'd had it way rougher than I had on this one, no matter how I felt.

"I don't know, Donovan. I won't mind never hearing about one more poor girl who got involved with this guy, but I'm okay either way," she said. "But then, hey, I'm already in therapy now," she chuckled without humor.

"Listen, I might change my mind when I talk to her, but I'm going to go see Mrs. Hollander and tell her we're resigning the case," I said.

On the drive over to the Hollanders' house, I thought back on all the women who'd been hurt by this guy. Logically, I knew that more than likely something had happened to Roger Hollander when he was young to make him like he was, but there would never be a time to rectify that. Now there was only dealing with the repercussions of what he had done.

All those women at the hands of a freak. The consistency was as remarkable as it was disturbing.

I called Mrs. Hollander while I was on the way and asked if I could come over. She asked if there had been a break. I told her there was a weird one, unrelated to the case, but otherwise I'd just fill her in when I got there.

We sat at her kitchen table. She was having coffee, but I just asked for a glass of water. I told her that we had followed up on the police handling of the matter and that as we had discussed they were still actively pursuing the case. I told her that Detective Baker particularly had a high personal regard for her. I told her that her son had several relationships, but no information had panned out from them. I told her about Larry Green and how it turned out to have nothing to do with the case and that now he worked for the Feds.

Then I told her that I believed it was unlikely we could get any further on the case and that it would be unethical for us to keep taking her money. The police would continue searching reports for other, similar homicides. Chances were that if the killer acted once in such a fashion, he or she would do so again.

In the end, she thanked me for trying and told me to send the bill to her as soon as possible, which I promised to do. She asked me to reconsider. I told her that I had really thought about it and that we could use the money, but it would just be wrong to continue when I had no real expectation of solving it. I told her I could recommend another agency, but that I really hoped that she would at least consider not doing so.

"Goodbye, Mrs. Hollander. I really am sorry for your loss," I said.

CHAPTER 57

Calling something an emotional roller coaster implies that like an actual roller coaster there would be some upward movement preceding or following the corresponding downward movement. In that sense, I couldn't accurately call today an emotional roller coaster. It had been either level or distinctly downward, like an Acme rocket sled in a Road Runner cartoon. And that pretty much made me Wile E. Coyote, Super Genius.

When I pulled up at Digs' place, I realized I was still wearing my ankle holster and back-up weapon. I reached down, undid it, went to the trunk and got my lock box. I opened it up, placed the gun and holster in it, closed and locked it, and then slid it under the seat. I locked the car, went to the front door, and let myself in.

Digs was standing at the kitchen counter chopping some celery. A pot was on the stove with something boiling. Whatever it was smelled good. She stopped chopping when she saw me and she smiled.

"Hey, you're supposed to say 'Hi, honey! I'm home!' or something like that, aren't you?" she asked. She set down the knife, wiped her hands on a kitchen towel, came over to me and gave me a big hug.

"I had a rotten day," I said and sat down at the table.

She eyed the timer on the stove and sat down slightly across from me.

"What happened?"

"It was just a mess. I don't like getting emotionally invested in one outcome. It makes me not open to whatever really happened," I said. "I need to ask you a really insensitive question."

"Shoot," she said.

"Have you ever been pregnant?"

She made an odd face – her surprised by a weird question face, and then smiled.

"No, I have never been pregnant, Donovan," she said.

The air went out of me like being punched in the gut. I blinked and kept my eyes closed for a moment.

"Why did you ask that?"

"I have one more question," I said because it was easier to say I had the question than it was to actually get the words out.

"Why did you kill Roger Hollander?"

I stared at her and she stared back. It was like a staring contest, only in this case if either of us blinked our dreams, our lives were over.

Of course, we both blinked.

"I'm sorry," she said very quietly, lowering her head.

"Digs, I'm not saying the son of a bitch didn't deserve it. From everything I've learned, he not only deserved it, he deserved worse. But you have to tell me what happened," I said.

"Rhonda. My niece. He hired my niece for his store at the mall. She's just 16 and she's beautiful. She doesn't have my last name, so he didn't know, or at least I don't think he did. I couldn't stand the thought of it."

"All things being equal, I probably would have done the same thing. How did it happen?"

"Talking to him, lying to him and telling him that I remembered him so fondly, it was everything I could do not to vomit, but I've been through enough therapy that I at least knew what he wanted to hear. It hadn't stopped him from hitting on my niece earlier that day, but it got me in close to him. All I had to do was dress like a teenager and say the right things," she said. "As far as actually stabbing him, it was like once I started I couldn't stop. I wish I was sorry about killing him. The only thing I'm sorry about is lying to you."

Everything felt heavy. Everything. My head, my hands, the room around us, even breathing.

"Was any of this real?"

"Donovan, all of this was real. I know given what I've done and how I lied... I know you can't believe me now, but I meant everything I said to you."

I believed her. That made it worse.

By that point I knew my instincts had been fouled up for weeks, since I saw her again, but I believed her. I knew I wanted to, so I tried not to, but I did. I stood up and so did she. She hugged me fiercely and started crying. I walked into the kitchen, turned off whatever was boiling, and then took her into the living room. We sat together on the sofa and she cried for a long time.

After a while, she went to sleep. I called my regular attorney, Harry Fenton, and asked him who he'd use for a criminal defense. He gave me Franklin Mathews, a guy I had seen on TV. Mathews came off smug, like a jerk, and I balked.

"He may act like one of those TV bozos when he's on TV, but he's a shark," my guy said. "Tell him I sent you. He owes me a couple."

I did that. I gave Mathews a quick rundown and told him that Digs would be ready to surrender to authorities in Hurst tomorrow morning. I told him briefly of my newfound relationship with the DA and that I planned to use that for all it was worth.

After that, I called Molsby. I told him that Mathews would be in touch and we'd be surrendering someone in conjunction with the death of Roger Hollander. I didn't tell him that it was Digs, who he had met years back, and I didn't tell him about Baker's issues. If that came out or didn't, that wasn't my call unless someone asked me specifically about it. In that case, the chips would fall where they might.

The next call I made was the first one I should have made, Michelle. When she answered, the wind went out of me again.

"It was Digs," I said before the voice went out of me. Then I stood there while Michelle called my name over and over.

* * *

When Digs woke up, I was sitting on the bed next to her. She smiled, having forgotten for the kindest of moments. Then she remembered. She put her hand on me.

"It's over, isn't it?"

I nodded.

"Will you go with me and the lawyer when I turn myself in?" she asked.

I nodded again.

"I don't want it to be over," she said.

"I know," I said. "Me either."

EPILOGUE

TWO MONTHS LATER

Things were different, as things often are. Even though there was no sensational trial, Digs' plea deal and sentencing had brought a small media stir. What came with that was a couple of solid cases, a handful of minor ones, and three different businesses putting us on retainer. Michelle was busy and happy, Tyler was working for us almost full-time, and Laura was still helping out part-time. I was surrounded not just by colleagues, but by friends.

But the color had gone out of my world. Things were simply more black and white and gray. It felt like a chapter had been ripped out of my favorite book and that I kept checking it to see if it had come back. It hadn't.

My regular gym schedule was my finger-hold on sanity. I had done a long workout after leaving the office and it was now approaching 7 p.m. I was leaving the gym and headed for home. I didn't have any plans and didn't plan on having any plans.

My phone rang and without looking I answered it.

"Donovan Bay," I said.

"Donovan Bay, the famous private investigator?" said

Kayla Singh with mock excitement. "Is it really you?"

"Sorry I haven't called back," I said.

"Well, according to radio, TV, newspapers and the internet, you've been busy," she said.

"How are you doing, Kayla?"

"Good. No, great. For the first time in a long time. Thanks for hooking me up with Dr. Sinclair. She's fantastic," she said.

"I'm really glad to hear that."

"But what about you? You don't sound like yourself?"

"Oh, I'm okay. Just tired."

"Well, I hope you're not too tired to come out to Vision Convoy tonight, and I really apologize for the short notice, but I got some excellent news and wanted to share it with someone cool. We're actually going to be recording a couple of tracks at tonight's show and we're really close to signing with what passes for a major label," she said. "And I'd really like to see you."

I congratulated her on the news and told her I was very happy for her, but begged off seeing her this evening. I was just exhausted and the show started in an hour.

She sounded genuinely disappointed, but told me she'd leave me a VIP ticket at the will call window just in case, and that I was certainly welcome to call her whenever I could make it another time. I told her I would and we hung up.

I got in the car and headed for my place with all of its silence.

An hour later I was in the front row at Vision Convoy when Kayla and Those Meddling Kids went on. Even if I didn't know why.

ADDITIONAL THANKS

The author extends a special thank-you to

Josh Geppi • **Larry Green** • **Michael Solof** • **Jeff Veytia**

---

for their support of this project.

SPOT ILLUSTRATIONS

in the Deluxe Edition

Donovan Bay & Michelle Benson **by Billy Tucci**

Sgt. Molsby **by John K. Snyder III**

Jennifer "Digs" O'Conner **by Mary Wilshire**

Jean Hollander **by Alex Saviuk**

Laura Field **by Chris Evenhuis**

Tyler Newsup **by Ed Catto**

Kaylah Singh **by Joe James**

Ginger Baker **by Mark Wheatley**

Colors **by Brian Miller/Hi-Fi Colour Design**, except

Laura Field **by Chris Evenhuis**

Ginger Baker **by Mark Wheatley**

ABOUT THE AUTHOR

J.C. VAUGHN has written literally thousands of articles, scores of comic books, and a number of screenplays. He has contributed to, edited, or originated more than 50 non-fiction books. This is his first novel.

In comics, he created or co-created *Zombie-Proof* (with Vincent Spencer), *Vampire, PA*, *The Flight*, and *Antiques: The Comic Strip* with Brendon & Brian Fraim, and *Return of the Human* with Mark Wheatley, as well as *Bedtime Stories for Impressionable Children*, *McCandless & Company*, and others.

With fellow *Stargate Atlantis* and *Stargate Universe* scribe Mark L. Haynes, he wrote three original graphic novels and a mini-based based on the Fox TV series *24*. He also has written or co-written *Shi* (with Billy Tucci), *Mighty Samson* (with Jim Shooter), *Cory Doctorow's Futuristic Tales of the Here & Now*, Blue Beetle in the *DC Universe Holiday Special 2008*, and *Battlestar Galactica*.

He is best known as the Vice-President of Publishing for Gemstone Publishing, the home of *The Overstreet Comic Book Price Guide*. He is presently developing a pilot for Roddenberry Entertainment with Mark L. Haynes, and several other projects, including a second novel.

Beginning on the following page is the first Michelle Benson solo story. It was written after the first draft of **Second Wednesday** was completed, when it became clear that Michelle, as a character, had more to say than I first expected.

– JCV

SATURDAY NIGHT

(THE USUAL)

By J.C. Vaughn

Clarence "Red" Castleman was a huge jerk, literally. And when I say "literally," I don't mean "figuratively," which is what most people mean when they say "literally." He was about 6'6" tall, over 350 pounds, snarled when he spoke, used his considerable height and weight to intimidate people, and he genuinely smelled really bad. Literally. Really. Bad.

With his palms down, he leaned on the bar and ordered – as in demanded – another whiskey. The bartender, a wiry guy named Myron Boddicker, jumped to it. He did a halfway good impression of someone who wasn't afraid, but once Clarence turned away Myron clearly looked relieved to have survived another encounter with him…but also aware that he might be back for another drink soon.

A well-founded general unease, I think it would be safe to say.

The Barber Shop, which was about the stupidest name for a bar I could imagine, was packed with biker-types and men who worked the oil rigs. Given the opportunity, they were a pretty rowdy bunch and the two groups did not always mix well, but tonight it seemed like both sides were sort of watching Clarence and waiting to see what would happen. He just had that air about him.

And about six whiskeys in him so far…

Business at The Barber Shop was good. Permits for drilling new oil wells had more than doubled in the last couple of years. They had seriously dropped off for a few years, but they were now on their way back again. That meant money was flowing in this part of the Permean Basin, where west Texas meets southeast New Mexico.

The understaffed team of waitresses cut pathways between the tables and groups of standing men, trays of beers and other drinks held high on their outstretched arms, rushing back and forth. Even so, there were plenty of customers in line at the bar to get drinks for themselves.

"Another round, honey," said one of the roughnecks as I approached his table. He wasn't obnoxious about it, just a little toasted.

"Sure thing," I smiled. "You driving tonight, honey?"

"Dave here is our designated driver, sweet thing," Toasted pointed with his thumb to the guy on his right, and Dave was actually sipping an iced tea. Good for him.

"It's taking me so long to get back to you guys, how about I bring you each two this trip?"

This brought cheers followed by a few friendly whistles as I made a show of turning around and walking back to the bar. These were raucous guys, but they weren't bad men.

I cast an eye toward where Clarence had occupied a table meant for six with just two other men. The place was nearly packed, but no one seemed like they were going to complain about it or ask to share his table.

Janine Davis, one of the other waitresses, sat yet another whiskey down in front of him and picked up his empty glass. There was no way to hear across the bar over the noise, but he clearly ordered another – good – and then he slapped her on the rear end as she turned to walk away.

He howled with laughter. Janine just looked embarrassed as she headed back to the bar.

It wouldn't be long now. Big guy or not, enough

whiskey and he'd go down a lot easier. I had slipped Myron Boddicker there behind the bar a crisp new hundred-dollar bill to make all of Clarence's drinks doubles.

Janine reached the bar, placed her order with Myron, and looked back over her shoulder as she waited for it. She watched Clarence make a menacing face at one of the guys he was sitting with and then burst out laughing again. The other guy looked relieved to have been spared for another moment. Myron put the drink on her tray and she headed back through the sea of thirsty, hard-drinking oil men.

Inez Santiago, another of the waitresses, with a full tray of drinks held aloft by one hand and necks of three bottles of beer between her fingers on the other, looked at Janine carrying the one drink across the room and started to shake her head.

"You know, normally that would just piss me off, but she's got her hands full with that guy. He's only been coming here for about a week, but he's trouble," she said over the noise as she turned to dive back into the fray.

"Thanks for the warning," I said as Myron loaded too many bottles to count on my tray.

The evening progressed. We continued to make the rounds as the men sat or stood in groups, enjoying themselves, boasting and laughing and bitching and moaning about the day's events. Some came and some left, but most of them stayed and drank.

Clarence didn't just keep up the pace; he set it.

On one trip back to the bar, I timed it so I met up with Janine.

"Why don't I take King Kong his whiskey this time?" I asked. "You look like you could use a break."

The combination of disbelief and relief on her face said enough.

"Take a round of long necks to those guys at table 19. I'll take care of the Incredible Hulk's dumber, smellier brother."

I couldn't hear her, but I could read the "Thank-you" on her lips as I walked toward Clarence with his whiskey on my tray.

When I slammed the drink down in front of him, he turned his attention from one of his tablemates to me. He looked down and saw that some of it had spilled.

"You spilled my drink!" he growled.

"I spilled your drink," I said.

"You're not Janine."

"I'm not Janine."

"You're just repeating what I say," he said.

"I'm just repeating what you say."

He stood up, sending his chair flying backwards. It fell over onto the cement floor. The noise in the room didn't exactly stop, but it sure got a whole lot quieter.

Clarence was indeed huge. He had 14 inches and about 230 pounds on me. Despite what you think you learned from Lara Croft, Tomb Raider, all things being equal, a woman my size is simply not going to be able to take a man his size. Even a wobbly man his size, as he now was.

So, the hell with letting things be equal.

I let my tray drop to the ground. When his eyes darted

to it, I spun and kicked full extension with my left leg into his gut, giving him everything I had. Before he could react, I turned my torso toward him and connected my fist with his Adam's apple. His hands moved up from his stomach to his throat.

I reached into my apron, grabbed the handle, pressed my taser straight into his crotch, and let him have it. After a moment (or three), I stopped. I stepped back and watched him fall flat on his face. It was okay, though. The cement floor broke his fall.

The sound of his impact made me aware that it had gotten extremely quiet in the place, except for Toasted and Dave saying "Whoa..." in unison. I turned to look at Clarence's tablemates, but they each gave me their best "We don't know that guy" looks.

I walked over to Toasted and Dave's table and asked if they'd mind helping me get Clarence into my car. They started to stand up, but then Toasted asked, "Isn't that kidnapping or something?"

"My name is Michelle Benson. I'm a licensed private investigator and bounty hunter," I said. I even flashed them my ID like I was on TV or something. "Clarence here is wanted on multiple charges in Tarrant and Dallas counties, and he skipped out on his bail bondsman. That's where I came in."

That seemed good enough for the men. Together they picked him up and carried him outside. I cuffed his hands behind his back and the guys worked him into the backseat of my rental. He was still out of it, so I thanked the guys and went back into the bar to turn in my apron.

"That was something," Myron said. Janine and Inez agreed, it was something. Toasted and Dave and their friends had followed me back in. I think Toasted was sort of smitten with me.

I looked at my watch. If I made great time, it would take me half a day to get back to Fort Worth. I said my goodbyes, walked out, climbed in the car, sat my taser on the front passenger seat, made sure my gun was still in the glove box, and headed for home.